Throw the Elbow

An April May Snow

Southern Paranormal Fiction Thriller

By

M. Scott Swanson

April May Snow Titles

Foolish Aspirations
Foolish Beliefs
Foolish Cravings
Foolish Desires
Foolish Expectations
Foolish Fantasies
Foolish Games

Seven Title Prequel Series

Throw the Bouquet

Throw the Cap

Throw the Dice

Throw the Elbow

Throw the Fastball

Throw the Gauntlet

Throw the Hissy

Never miss an April May Snow release.

Join the reader's club!

www.mscottswanson.com

Cousins are sisters you never had.

– Reah Glowstorl

Chapter 1

I guard our drinks while Trisha leaves for the ladies' room.

Crossing my arms, I close my eyes and sway to the cover band's poor rendition of "Cheeseburger in Paradise." I'm in paradise.

A cheeseburger would be good about now, too.

Bless it. What time is it anyway?

I pull my phone to me, wiping the condensation twice before my phone confirms it's me—April.

It is close to midnight. That surprises me since I feel like Trisha and I just arrived at Three Sheets to the Wind, a beach bar in Pensacola, Florida.

My cousin Trisha and I tend to lose track of time on the rare occasions we manage to get together. If Trisha were not my cousin, she would be my best girlfriend. Instead, she is family. Which takes a lot of pressure off me since if I ever accidentally say something that hurts her feelings, she can't ghost me. She is stuck with me for life.

Trisha saved my life with a well-timed phone call three days ago. Well, not literally saved my life. But if she had not called, I would be in my lonely Tuscaloosa apartment feeling sorry for myself and close to dying of boredom. Instead, I'm sitting at a beachside bar, pushing my toes into the cool sand as the fickle breeze whips my beach hair off my bare shoulders.

It's a tough gig. But somebody has to do it.

I pick up my rum runner and take another sip of the fruity concoction that opens my sinuses as the excess coconut rum hits the back of my palate. Lord, this must be a three-shot rum runner. It tastes about right.

The last thing I need is more alcohol. I already have a comfortable buzz. Still, it's like drinking Kool-Aid now, and my self-discipline has disappeared.

"You are so hot I think I might have to go skinny dipping to cool off."

I look up in a state of confusion. There is a dude I don't know, standing in front of my table with a goofy look of expectation. Despite the mid-seventy-degree temperature and the darkness of the bar, he wears a heavy nylon flight jacket and dark aviator sunglasses.

I'm surprised he didn't crack a kneecap against a chair on his way to my table. He can't possibly see a thing.

My dulled brain finally processes what he said, and I turn my head to see who he is talking to. Nope, the bamboo wall is all there is behind me. Crap. He is talking to me.

"I'd keep them on if I were you. Most folks look better with their clothes on," I say with a healthy dose of snark.

"I would love to test that theory with you."

Well, peaches. I walked into that one. But who would have guessed a boy with that goofy grin would be quick-witted?

"I'm not sure my boyfriend would appreciate that."

Mr. Goofy Grin hooks the thumb of his free hand in his front jeans pocket. He casually points his beer toward the ladies' room. "Her? She can come, too. I'm a progressive thinker."

Right. I don't want to take the time to explain to him how he is the antithesis of progressive.

"Come on, it would be fun."

Like a root canal, I'm sure. This dude is seriously messing with my buzz. "Listen, my girlfriend just needs to talk tonight. *Girl* talk."

"Yeah, sure. I understand. But a little fun never hurts, either."

I'm sure he can use a swim to cool off. He must be sweating profusely under that heavy flight jacket. Even if I were inclined to take a dip, I watched *Jaws* when I was younger. I'm aware the big sharks eat at night. "Thanks, but we are pretty close to calling it a night."

"Come on! It will be fun. Besides, you can tell all your friends tomorrow you went swimming with a Blue Angel."

My family holds the Blue Angels in high esteem. It's one of the reasons we love Pensacola. A Blue Angel flyby while on the beach nursing a cold beer is considered a top highlight of any summer.

I size Mr. Goofy Grin up. While many pilots are shorter than my brothers due to cockpit restrictions, I find him lacking. For one thing, he doesn't seem to have the muscle tone required to pull six G's and not pass out. Second, I would be crushed to think a Blue Angel is this lame. "As attractive as that sounds, I'm going to pass."

His hand shoots forward, and he lifts my drink. Instinctively, I grab his hand. "What do you think you're doing?"

His emotions are highly charged, as are mine. The energy connection between us opens like a flood gate. So many stimuli flow to me. I'm slammed hard with a momentary bout of vertigo.

"I was going to buy you a fresh drink. What do you have?"

"Enough. That's what I have." I take my drink back with my other hand. "Didn't your mama teach you it's bad manners to grab somebody's drink?"

He offers me a broad smile. I'm sure he thinks he is sexy. "You are going to turn down a free drink from a Blue Angel?"

All right, now I've lost my patience. The dude has messed up my buzz, and he needs to get out of my space. "You are not a Blue Angel. You bought that jacket online. In fact, you're not even a pilot.

"You work as a buffer operator cleaning floors at the local VA. You used that pickup line about the Blue Angels the first time six months ago with a girl named Leslie who was too ditzy to know the difference, and you have been using it ever since."

"Her name was Lauren."

"Yeah, whatever." I take the last sip from my drink, making a pronounced slurping noise.

The conversation finally seems to catch up with him as his eyes open wider. "How do you know?"

He turns a chair around and straddles it backward. Precisely the opposite reaction I was hoping for with my psychic parlor trick.

"Do I know you?" he asks.

"You wish." I don't want to be rude. Still, he is annoying the stew out of me.

"How do you know all that about me?"

"I'm psychic."

"Really? Wow. So, do you like work for the police? I have seen shows where the psychics work for the police, solving cases and stuff."

"No, I'm actually a lawyer." I look toward the ladies' room, willing Trisha to come and save me.

Goofy shakes a finger at me. "Ah." He laughs. "You had me going there. I almost believed you until you threw in the lawyer part. A girl as beautiful as you does not need to become a lawyer. Heck, you would just marry one."

I'm stunned and speechless for more than a few reasons. I should be offended by Goofy's statement, but the sincerity of his backhanded compliment just makes me roll my eyes.

He taps the fingers of his right hand on the back of the chair. I notice the tattoos "N-E-E-D-4" spread across each knuckle, the '4' being on the side of his thumb. Like an idiot, I check his left hand and find the answer. "S-P-E-E-D." I'm so sure.

Goofy notices me looking and says, "True story. I have the need."

So far, I have tried everything, including the direct brush-off. I like to use the delay and depart strategy when all else fails. It is a favorite for folks like me who don't want to disappoint other people—at least not face to face.

I lean forward and favor him with a smile. "I can't promise anything because my friend is sort of shy. But give me a little time to try and talk her into going swimming. I will give you a signal if she is up for a swim."

His face twitches into a broad smile once his mind processes what I'm telling him. "Oh. All right."

I raise my eyebrows, and he shudders into action. "I need to go back to the bar?"

"That would be best."

Goofy nods. "Yeah, cool." He starts and looks back with a snap of his neck. "Don't forget to give me a signal. Oh yeah, and my name is Ace. What is yours?"

Of course, your name is Ace, Mr. Not-A-Pilot. "Destiny." I'm not giving this joker my name.

His expression brightens. "I hope it is."

I think I'm gonna be sick.

"Signal me," he repeats.

"I will," I promise with a finger wave. Geez. Trisha and I have about a fifty-fifty chance of getting out of this barroom unnoticed.

Ace takes a spot at the bar. As he turns to order another beer, I notice if his jeans were any tighter, they would be body paint. Begrudgingly I admit he does have a really cute tush.

He turns and leans against the bar. Lifting his longneck bottle, he points the top toward me and winks.

Yeah, he is locked on like a heat-seeking missile. Trisha and I now have a five-percent chance of leaving without a confrontation. Our odds are getting lower by the minute.

Trisha returns from the ladies' room. As she starts to sit, I stop her. "Tell me you want to stand at the bar."

"Why?" she asks.

"Don't look, but we have an admirer at the bar..."

Trisha cranes her neck to scan the bar. "Which one?"

"The goofball in the flight jacket," I huff.

"He is sorta cute."

Please. Trisha seriously needs to raise her cute-guy bar a notch or two.

"Are we going to talk to him?"

"No, he is a pest. If we don't move to the bar, he will sit down at our table. Trust me."

Trisha does not conceal her disappointment but lifts her drink and follows me to the bar. I feel guilty. I'm cutting into Trisha's fun. That is the last thing I want to do since her life has been vastly different from mine. She rarely has the opportunity to socialize.

"If you really want to talk to him—"

"I'm good." She leans against the bar.

Trisha is lying, and I feel even worse. "He is kinda cute."

"It's probably just the rum glasses we are wearing. Most likely, you just saved me from being a single mom."

Trisha's humor is so dry I wait for her grin before I'm sure she is joking. "I would like a nephew."

"I would like to be able to tell your nephew his last name." She takes a sip of her drink.

"It is late. Should you call your dad?"

"I texted him. He told me not to expect him back. He has an all-nighter."

I jerk to the side and drawl out, "Eww—"

Trisha squints as she studies me. She bursts into a delightful bout of laughter. "Card game—he and his Navy buddies hooked up tonight. Besides, grow up. Old folks do it, too."

"That doesn't mean I want to talk about it."

She props her chin on her fists. "Probably more than folks our age nowadays. With stalkers, creeps, and STDs to worry about."

"Is your love life that good?" Between her full-time job and law school at night, I know it must be hard for Trisha to make time for dating. It has been years since she mentioned a meaningful relationship.

"Nonexistent. What about you?"

"Oh, you know. I get plenty of opportunities. Still, being I'm starting a new career, I'll probably just focus on April for a while." The last part is truthful.

She stares at me for a moment as if searching for something. "You have always been lucky like that. I'm just so lonely at times.

I would do anything to meet up with someone I really like. Sometimes I think I would rather marry a really kind guy than be a lawyer."

"Such blasphemy," I joke.

"You don't understand what it is like to be lonely."

Trisha does not know. If she didn't invite me to the beach, I would be sitting in my apartment, rotating between salty and sweet junk foods while counting all the ways my life bites. Experience has taught me no matter how much I like cookie dough ice cream and Cool Ranch Doritos, an excess of that combination always makes me sick. Then what?

Forget about pride and reputation. It is time I come clean. If I can't be vulnerable with my cousin, what point is family? I should be able to share everything with her.

"Listen, Trisha. This is not easy for me to admit. You know how you act like I have all these hot guys tripping over themselves to be with me? The truth of the matter is—"

A cold hand glides over my bare shoulder. "Are we ready to get naked and go for a swim, girls?"

Rage flames through me for the rude interruption during my most vulnerable moment. I momentarily lose control of my body. Specifically, my elbow. I do intentionally throw my elbow. It is on the worn oak bar top one second and behind me the next moment, barreling into a mound of taut flesh.

There is a loud grunt. The hand on my shoulder slides a trail down my back.

Trisha's eyes open wide. She makes a yelp as her focus goes behind me.

I turn in time to watch Ace drop to one knee in the sand as he clutches at his sternum. His mouth opens and closes like a goldfish out of water, gulping for air.

Fudge nut!

I bend over and put my hand on his shoulder. "I'm sorry."

"April!" Trisha looks horrified as she squats to examine Ace's condition.

"What? It was an accident."

"Hey, buddy. You okay?" I ask hopefully.

Tears leak from the side of Ace's eyes, and his face color has blanched. He stretches his neck, and I hear him draw in a single, ragged breath.

He is breathing. I feel better already. At least I didn't kill him. Right?

Trisha helps Ace to his feet. Leaning across him, she wipes the white sand from the knees of his painted-on jeans.

"There you go," she coos. "Take your time."

I'm standing here like a bump on a log. I guess I'm shocked I could do that much damage with my elbow. The need to at least seem caring and helpful kicks into gear. "Do you need some water?"

Ace's accusing stare makes me lean back. He is not going to let bygones be bygones just yet.

Trisha slips his arm over her shoulder. She helps Ace to a chair at the table we just left. Lord, her nurturing state is off the chart. This is so unnecessary. He is obviously okay.

"April, get him water."

"A Corona," Ace says.

I bite my tongue. After giving Ace spontaneous chest compression, I can play nice and buy the boy a beer.

I return with a beer to find Trisha's chair pulled so close to Ace their knees touch. She continues to ask him questions about his health. I cross her attentive stare with the cold bottle, setting it on the table with a thud.

Ace's brow knits. "No lime?"

Are you kidding me? The nerve of this guy.

"Get him a lime, April," Trisha says as she places her hand on his knee.

My jaw falls open momentarily before I gather my senses and stomp back to the bar to find a lime. I also order a giant margarita for me and a coffee for Trisha. As I return to the table, I slide the cup of coffee toward Trisha. She frowns at me without comment.

Ace has finished his beer. So much for the lime.

"Ace is a Blue Angel. Isn't that the coolest?"

"It's no big deal." Ace delivers an "aw shucks" expression.

"It is too. I can't imagine strapping myself into one of those scary machines."

I'm positive Ace has an equally tough time imagining getting into a fighter jet. Given the closest he has been to one is while watching them streak across the horizon as he sat on the beach, I struggle to contain my laugh.

Curious, I study Trisha to see if she is buying what Ace is selling or just being pleasant. Her eyes are wide, lips slightly parted, as she leans closer to Ace. Not only is Trisha buying his story, but she is also Ace's newest jet jockey groupie.

You know what? What does it hurt to let her talk to a guy tonight who finds her attractive? Heck, it will give her confidence the boost she has been needing.

Who cares if I know Ace is a loser? As long as I'm with Trisha, she can't end up doing anything stupid with a wannabe flyboy.

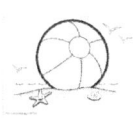

Chapter 2

Begrudgingly, I must admit Ace is an intelligent guy and an excellent conversationalist if you allow him to become comfortable. If he weren't so full of bull malarkey, I might even like him.

The chemistry between Ace and Trisha is undeniable. Consequently, it's time I do my job as a goalkeeper and put an end to their little affair before things go too far.

I open my mouth to announce to Trisha I want to hunt down a late-night dinner. My words catch in my throat as a foreboding wave of evil disrupts the energy in the bar.

A tall, harshly attractive couple enters the bar. My skin prickles as if a thousand spiders are crawling on my neck and face.

The woman is tall with a formidable build. Her makeup is so thick, it appears as if she applied it with a spatula. The bar lights reflect off her bright-red, uniformly dyed hair.

Red's escort, a block-jawed man, easily stands six foot five. He wears a thin black cotton T-shirt fighting to conceal his steroid-engorged muscles. Steroid scans the barroom with a predatory stare that sends the spiders scurrying from my skin. My muscles simultaneously lock into a catatonic state as my "freeze" instinct clunks into gear.

Bad news.

There is one positive aspect of being cursed with psychic abilities. I own a sixth sense that allows me to identify individuals who are naturally distasteful to be around. The skill affords me the ability to simply avoid unpleasant people. Experience has proven to me you can't change them, and quite frankly, I don't have the time to waste on mean people.

This couple is beyond the standard mean. The malicious energy radiating from them signals the couple is capable of evil deeds and would actually enjoy them.

I watch the couple cruise to a table positioned in the far corner. I can't help it. I have some voyeuristic tendencies, which only compound my overactive curiosity. I notice their body language toward one another is no better than the evil energy they're secreting.

"So, what do you think?"

Trisha draws my attention back to our table. "About what?"

"Do you want to go for a swim?"

"Have you never seen *Jaws*?" I ask with a heavy tone of incredulity.

"What's that?" Ace asks.

I acknowledge the blank look on both their faces and realize not everyone has parents who insist their children watch movies from the parents' youths. "Never mind. No. I don't want to go swimming. But I really could use something to eat."

"Yeah, I'll second that," Ace interjects as if I invited him.

"What's open this hour?" Trisha asks.

"Waffle House."

"Yeah, I can go for a waffle." Trisha gets an odd dreamy look in her eyes.

"Man, I could really use some smothered and covered hash browns about now," Ace kicks in.

I'm not about to let Ace tag along and ruin my extra greasy fried hamburger I'm constructing in my mind. "Ace, Trisha and I will probably just go by ourselves."

Immediately I regret my honesty. Ace's expression looks like I caught him a second time with my elbow.

Trisha leans back as if I slapped her. Great. I'm about to receive a lecture by Mom Trisha.

"April, the least we can do is buy Ace dinner after the near-death experience you put him through."

"Wait. She keeps calling you April. I thought your name was Destiny." Ace scratches his head as he stares at me.

It's clear my destiny is to eat my hamburger while listening to Ace yammer all night about his fantasy career. I better take some Pepcid AC now, so I don't develop indigestion. "Fine, he can come."

"Y'all give me a minute. I have to go to the ladies' room," Trisha says.

"Good Lord. Girl, are you okay?" I ask.

She glares pointedly at me, picks up her purse, and walks toward the ladies' room. Ace and I sit in awkward silence for a moment.

"So, your name is not Destiny?"

"I can't believe you believed it was," I grumble.

Ace appears crestfallen. "Well, I thought it was a really cool name."

"I would say I hate to disappoint you, but we don't know each other like that. While we are on the topic of disappointments, so we can manage expectations, we are going to go and have something to eat. Then you are going to say goodbye."

"Why?"

I raise my hands, palms up. "Because this isn't going anywhere."

Ace points toward the ladies' room. "But I like her."

"Which is precisely why this isn't going anywhere, Mr. Fake Blue Angel Man. You can't start a relationship on a lie and expect it to last."

Ace considers my comment for a moment. "Interesting. I have always wondered how I'm supposed to move the relationship to the next step. I always knew that sooner or later the girl would figure out I'm not a Blue Angel."

Bless it. If the world were full of more intelligent people, there would be a lot fewer reasons to drink. I have long since finished my drink. I steal a sip off Trisha's leftover rum runner, then gag. She was drinking a Shirley Temple before I bought her the coffee.

"Tell me. Seeing as you're a girl."

I cock my head to the side and favor Ace a "really dude" glare.

"How do I get girls interested in me if I'm not a fighter jet pilot?"

Ace is so giving me a headache. "I don't know, Ace. Maybe by being yourself. The first thing to understand is not every girl will be attracted to you or find you interesting. The trick is not to get hung up on those who don't mesh with you. You don't need every girl to be interested. My daddy likes to say there is not a pot too crooked that a lid won't fit."

Ace's mouth falls open as his eyes draw together. "Huh?"

I may yank Trisha baldheaded for inviting Ace to dinner. "It means there is somebody out there for you."

Ace's confused look turns into a smile. "Cool."

I feel his presence before the shadow darkens Ace's face. "What did you say to my wife?"

The hostile tone is more of a command than a question. I look up at the steroid-enhanced beast of a man who walked in with the redhead earlier.

'Roid reaches down, grabs Ace by the front of his shirt, and yanks him to the edge of his chair. "Oh, you gonna be all quiet-like now? Now that I'm over here asking you a question. Let me tell you something, man. Your daddy should have taught you some manners. I guess I'm going to have to school you instead."

Ace clutches at our table as the giant man pulls him out of his chair. Our table tilts toward me, spilling Trisha's drink. I'm still trying to process what is happening with this huge man as Ace finally lets go of the table and scrambles to his feet.

"What are you talking about?" Ace asks.

That does seem to be the question of the moment. It defies all logic why this behemoth of a man has decided to rip Ace out of his chair. Sure, he can be annoying, but he hasn't even spoken to 'Roid or his bride.

Without answering Ace, 'Roid smashes his right fist into Ace's face. The knuckle-to-face contact is so loud I hear it over the cover band.

I recoil in shock. *What the heck!*

'Roid pulls his fist back and holds Ace at arm's length preparing for another punch. Ace's eyes cross as they focus on the heavy hand about to pummel him again.

"Stop it!" I scream.

"Somebody has to teach him some manners," 'Roid says before smashing his fist into Ace's nose.

Ace's nose ruptures. Blood streams across the front of his Blue Angels jacket. As his attacker holds Ace's limp body up, the whites of Ace's eyes show. I realize Ace is unconscious.

Sometimes I act without thinking about the consequences. This is one of those moments.

Grabbing the neck of Ace's empty Corona bottle, I scream, "I told you to leave him be!"

I swing the bottle, striking 'Roid on the forehead. The bottle explodes into hundreds of tiny shards of glass. Bits of glass strike my face as others land in my hair.

The beer bottle does not have the results I hoped. 'Roid releases Ace's shirt. Ace falls backward, and his head strikes the floor with a sickening thud. The mammoth man touches his forehead. He examines the trace of blood on the tips of his fingers with a slightly confused look.

I experience a totally inappropriate bout of giggles. I stare in wonderment at the man. How in tarnation is he still standing?

Staring at his forehead, I don't see 'Roid's hand move. His backhand connects with such force I spin around, landing against the table. My momentum pushes the table several feet before I regain my balance.

Man, that smarts!

My ears ring, and my vision darkens as I feel my consciousness fading. I don't dare blackout with this hateful man on a rampage.

I shake my head to clear the cobwebs. Gathering enough sense to turn, I see things have gone to heck in a handbasket.

'Roid is kicking Ace in the stomach. Ace is not responding. *Where is security?*

I take a split second to scan the room and solidify my resolve. There is a room full of people. They all shrink back in horror as the sheer violence 'Roid dishes out on Ace alarms them.

There will be no cavalry coming to our rescue.

My dad and brothers have drilled into my head an adage: "No pistol should be returned to its holster without being fired. Pistols are for protection, not brandishing. Especially if your assailant is big enough to wrestle the gun away from you."

I pull my two-shot forty-five ACP Bond Arms Backup with resolve and trepidation. Immediately I disregard my years of family firearm training.

"Stop, or I'll put you down, mister." My voice sounds incredibly calm. I believe that may have caught 'Roid's attention as much as the five-inch gun in my right hand.

He favors me with a crooked smile that sends shivers up my spine. "What do you expect to do with that pea shooter, little girl?"

"Hopefully, put it back in my purse once you come to your senses."

'Roid shakes his head as he smirks. "I'm gonna take that gun from you and shove it where only your boyfriend will find it."

The wisdom of my daddy and brothers' instruction is all too clear. Dread washes over me.

The only thing is, I have been hunting enough in my life to understand I despise killing things. Even evil men who deserve to be put down. "Oh my, that's original. I don't think I have ever heard that."

'Roid's eyes narrow. He leans forward as if he is preparing to bull rush me. Ace stirs at his feet, distracting him momentarily.

I take the opportunity to try one last thing to get out of the situation without having to drop this turkey. I fish in my purse with my left hand and pull out a twenty.

"Look, no harm done." I hold out the twenty in 'Roid's direction. "I don't know what he did to you, but have a couple of drinks on me and let's call it even."

"He disrespected my wife!" 'Roid yells.

It would not surprise me if Ace ever got in a situation where he mistakenly hit on a married woman. I so can see him asking another man's wife to go skinny-dipping.

Still, the fact is Ace was with me ever since 'Roid and his red-headed bride came into this establishment. Somebody may have hit on his wife. I'm confident it was not Ace.

"And you taught him a lesson. I'm sure he will not forget it." I hold 'Roid's level stare.

'Roid looks down at Ace. He seems to inventory the damage inflicted. He favors me a curt nod of his head as he steps forward and snatches the folded twenty-dollar bill from my hand.

'Roid turns toward the bar. Relief floods over me as my knees turn rubbery.

I push my Bond Arms Backup handgun back into my purse as a thick-bodied security guard approaches me.

The guard gestures with his finger. "No guns allowed in here. You will have to leave."

I lean over to help Ace up. "The least you can do is bring us some ice."

"What in the world have you done to him, April?"

Trisha's question makes me hang my head in frustration. "I didn't do anything."

Ace struggles to his feet with my help, and I sit him in a chair. I grab a handful of napkins and push them into his hand as I ease his head back. "Hold these to your nose until the bleeding stops."

"Miss, you will have to leave," the security guard says as his hand goes to the pepper spray on his belt.

"Oh, *please*. Where were you when all this was going down? Didn't I tell you to find some ice? We could leave a lot quicker if you got me the ice like I asked."

To my pleasant surprise, the guard turns and walks toward the bar. I assess the damage on Ace's face. Before I check his ribs, I already know it's terrible.

"We have got to get you to a hospital, Ace."

His eyes cross as he shakes his head. "No. I'm al—" He looks like he has lost something.

"Good?" I ask.

"That's the word I was looking for. I couldn't remember it," Ace slurs.

"April, I think he might have a concussion," Trisha frets.

"You think?" I say with a sarcastic tone.

I tilt Ace's chin down. The blood from his nose has slowed to a thin stream. Still, his eyes are so dilated he has no iris, only pupils. "Yeah. I'm not fond of hospitals either, Ace." We will not go into the reasons why I don't like hospitals. It would take too long to explain. "But you seriously need to be examined. I'm afraid you might have some brain swelling."

Ace tilts his head back as he pinches his nose. "Well, maybe it will finally fill the inside of my skull."

Bless it. How can you not like a guy who has a sense of humor after he just took a butt beating? "Still, we don't want to let it grow too large. If your head gets any bigger, you will never fit through barroom doors again."

"I'll go bring the car around," Trisha says.

"Girls, I appreciate the concern. But I think I'm going to be fine by the morning. I'll just walk home and sleep it off."

"Absolutely not. We are taking you to the hospital. Do not argue with me about this," I insist.

"You don't understand—okay, already—I don't have any health insurance. And I don't have a bunch of money to waste at the doctors."

I watch the frustration and what I can only take as shame torment Ace's expression. For the first time since he lied to me about being a Blue Angel, I feel his energy.

"Okay, no biggie." It is. That means Trisha and I must keep Ace awake until his eyes are normal. If he does not have massive swelling, that will lead to a seizure before he heals.

"April, we must take him to a hospital." Trisha's face is red. She gestures wildly with her as she speaks.

Great. I have one concussed fake Blue Angel and a cousin ten seconds away from a stroke. I just wanted to come here, have a couple of drinks, and push my toes through the sand. I must have been an awful person in my last life.

"Hey, there is no rush. Once we get some ice for Ace's nose, we'll go to Waffle House like we planned and have a pleasant late-night snack." I shrug. "By the time we finish eating, Ace will be feeling better. Then we can drive him home."

"I probably should call a ride. I don't think I can drive," Ace says. He slumps in his chair.

I shake Ace by the shoulder. "Wake up."

"You have been drinking like a fish. I'm not riding with you." Ace attempts to stare me level in the eyes. His right eye stares at my chin, and his left looks into my hairline.

"You are right. I'm not driving. We're going to let Miss Shirley Temple chauffeur us." I turn and glare at Trisha.

"We knew somebody was going to have to drive home. I sure wasn't going to wreck my dad's car," she protests.

The security guard finally shows up with the ice. I apply it to the back of Ace's neck as I lead him out of the bar.

With an overly official tone, the guard informs the three of us that we are not welcome back in the bar. I consider calling him a coward for not intervening in the earlier assault of Ace. Still, I have had enough unwinnable arguments for one night.

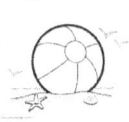

Chapter 3

There are three other cars in the Waffle House parking lot when we arrive. For Waffle House, that's a slow night at one AM.

We enter the restaurant and select a booth. Trisha sits first. Ace plops down on the bench beside her.

I crook a finger at him. "Uh-uh, big boy. You're gonna sit on the opposite side so I can keep an eye on you."

Ace stands with a tremendous show of effort and slides in on the other bench. Then I sit beside my cousin. Trisha and I take to staring at Ace.

"What?" he asks. "Y'all are looking at me as if I'm a two-headed turtle or something."

"I'm only making sure you are okay," Trisha says as she shrugs.

"I'm waiting to see if any gray matter leaks out your ears."

"April!" Trisha yells.

"I was just kidding." I point at Ace. "His coloring is already looking better. If he could just keep his eyes from doing that rolly thing with his eyes, I think he will be halfway to healed."

"I am feeling a little better," Ace agrees.

"And you will feel even better once you have eaten," Trisha says.

"So, inquiring minds want to know. Who was that guy, and why did he attack you?" I ask.

"His name is Champ Janikowski. His dad gave him the bar. I only know that because I have never seen him pay for a drink, and I asked about it one night."

That turkey took a twenty-dollar bill from me? When he gets his drinks for free?

"As for why he attacked me? I haven't a clue. I've never said two words to the guy. Before tonight I would have assumed he never even noticed me."

"Well, he noticed you tonight," I say sarcastically.

Ace rubs his side. "Yeah, and the dude wears some right pointy shoes."

"Boots," I correct.

The waitress interrupts our conversation to take our orders. I stick with the hamburger. Trisha and Ace have changed their minds from earlier and order omelets.

"You are not from around here. Where are your people?" I ask.

Ace chuckles. "My people?"

"Your family," Trisha translates.

"I grew up in Cleveland, Ohio. I was an electrical apprentice at a factory and got laid off. I signed up with a construction crew and ended up down here in the Panhandle wiring condos. When we finished the last high-rise, I decided I liked it here enough to stay."

"And tell everybody you are a Blue Angel," I add.

"Only because they are the area heroes. If I had settled in Boston, I would tell everybody I'm Tom Brady."

"You are not tall enough," I comment as I test the temperature of my coffee.

"People believe what they want to believe."

"It's still not nice to lie," Trisha grouses.

He stares at her before turning contrite. "You're right. It's not nice to lie."

"So, you don't find it even the least bit odd this guy you have never spoken to decides to knock you down and try to kick the stuffing out of you?"

"Of course, I think it's odd. It's just I don't know what caused him to go psycho on me. A stranger—"

"Something's definitely off with that," I mumble into my coffee. Either my new friend is not telling me the whole story, or Champ is confused and mistook Ace for somebody else.

Our food arrives. I table the discussion about the unfortunate events at the bar for now. I can study the details from here until eternity and not know what drove Champ to be so needlessly aggressive.

"I'm from Nashville," Trisha offers.

"I have always wanted to visit there. Maybe sometime soon, I can come up and visit you."

"Sure, I'll be your tour guide," she says.

We eat in companionable silence. We appear to be hungrier than we thought. Or being in life-or-death situations ramps up your appetite. Either way, the quiet gives me time to let the events of the night settle.

I still can't believe I had to pull my pocket cannon out tonight. I can't tell my brothers or dad, or they will give me an earful about the dangers of pulling a weapon without the intent of using it.

I have carried my firearm mostly to appease my daddy all these years. I hate to admit he was right. Still, after I shattered the bottle on Champ's head—if I had not had the weapon as a backup—I don't believe it would have played out as well for Ace and me. I think Ace would be dead, or maybe both of us. Depending on Champ's level of rage.

I can be primarily grateful about three things tonight.

Luckily, I carried my gun and Champ could be bought off for twenty dollars' worth of free liquor. That Ace appears to be regaining his faculties as we finish our late snack. Most of all that Trisha was in the bathroom and couldn't get in the way during the bar brawl.

All that luck has me feeling wild. "Can we go for a swim now?" I ask.

Ace narrows his eyes. "What about cramps. We just ate," Ace complains.

"What about the *Jaws* thing you were talking about? Isn't that a shark?" Trisha asks.

"That movie was about a great white. It was in the Atlantic. Everybody knows there are no great whites in the gulf." Maybe a few bull sharks.

"I thought somebody got bit at the start of the season," Ace says.

"They were probably taunting it. If you leave them alone, sharks won't bother you. Besides, the most a bull shark would do is bite you. It won't eat you," I say.

Neither seems to warm up to my rationalization. I choose to curtail any further discussion and grab the ticket, carrying it to the cashiers to pay.

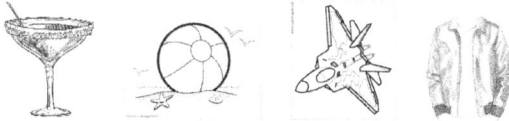

Trisha drives us to the beach. Even though I can tell by her body language she is less than enthused. Before I leave the vehicle, when she is not looking, I stow my handgun in the glove compartment.

The crisp, salty air sweeping off the gulf caresses my face as it lifts my hair off my back. I stroll onto the loosely packed dry sand that shimmers in the silvery moonlight. Stopping at the high tide mark, I pull my shirt over my head and kick off my shorts. Yeah, I'm going to do this.

"Woo-hoo," I holler as I run toward the foamy, iridescent water. I take two high steps into the surf. The sand drops from a three-foot ledge causing me to tumble forward into the tide.

Fudge, the water's cold tonight!

I stand. Pushing my hair away from my eyes, I wave at Trisha.

Ace is already standing next to my pile of clothes. He kicks off his shoes with lightning speed, pulls his shirt over his head, and shucks his shorts and underwear in one downward motion. He will regret that when he feels how cold the water is tonight.

"Come on, Trisha." I wave her on.

"I'm thinking about it."

"Mother of pearl, this is cold," Ace hollers as he slams into the surf.

"Cold enough to hurt your pride?" I tease.

Ace wades toward me. "Oh, you're gonna pay for that."

"No way, mister. Since you decided to swim commando, you will stay over there. You are not getting in my area."

"What? That ruins the fun."

"You better behave. I would hate to give you a second concussion tonight." My words sound slurred. I believe my face is frozen except for my teeth, which are chattering incessantly.

I look toward Trisha. She stands still at the top of the sand, watching us. "Quit thinking about it. Just grit your teeth and do it, Trisha."

She balances one foot on top of the other and crosses her arms across her chest. "What about the shark?"

"It got the day off. Nothing is going on out here," I say.

Trisha strips to her underwear. She pauses. "Are you sure there aren't any great whites, April?"

"Positive. Now get in here."

I'm out far enough that I can only touch the sand with my toes in the valleys of the waves as I float upward with each one rolling me toward the shore. Trisha half breaststrokes, half dog paddles her way toward me.

Ace swims closer, too. Fine. At least I will not have to yell over the surf. I can keep a closer watch on his condition this way.

"This is stupid, April May," Trisha chides me as she nears.

"Please. Don't act like you aren't enjoying it, Trisha. You need some excitement in your life."

"Not this kind." A wave slaps her in the face. Trisha coughs and spits. "Why I ever listen to you…"

"This isn't quite what I imagined it to be like," Ace complains.

"Few things in life are. Hey, I know. Let's play a game. Let's see who can tread water the longest without touching the bottom," I say.

"What does the winner get?" Ace asks.

"To win the game," I say in an exaggeratedly slow manner.

"Does floating count?" Trisha asks.

"Nope. Head and shoulders straight out of the water the whole time."

Trisha dog paddles momentarily before she treads water. "I don't know, April. I think I'm gonna catch hypothermia or something."

"I'll try," Ace volunteers.

Ace has more spunk than I thought. He might have had more fight in him at the bar if Champ had not ambushed him.

"Oh, all right," Trisha says.

We form a loose circle in the water. My toes do not touch even when I bob down on the wave trough. My entire body is as taut as a wound spring as I try to force the cold from my mind.

"Where you from anyway, April?" Ace slurs as he struggles to keep his chin above the surf.

"Georgia," I say. It's not a lie. That is where I'm moving to in a few weeks.

Ace nods his head. "How long will you be here?"

"Just a few days," I say quickly before Trisha gives him our address and itinerary for the next week.

We fall silent, sans the heavy breathing of our exertion to remain above the water. With the assistance of the salt in the water, I started the game at a controlled, relaxed pace. Now my legs are pumping frantically, and an uncomfortable burn is setting into my quads and buttocks.

"This sucks," Ace declares. "You win. I'm swimming in before I catch pneumonia."

"Not as sexy as you thought it would be?" I ask.

"Not at all. No wonder all those girls looked at me like I was crazy." He turns and swims freestyle toward the shore.

"What is he talking about?" Trisha asks.

"Ace tried to go all redneck Christian Grey on me back at the bar."

"What is Christian Grey?"

"You really need to read something other than the sweet romances, Trisha." I laugh, accidentally swallow part of a wave, and begin to choke.

Trisha swims closer. "Are you okay?"

"No touching, or you're disqualified," I say harsher than I meant.

"I will be sure to remember that if you slip under a wave."

A fresh jolt of tremors racks my body. "You don't have to get all testy."

"This is stupid. I'm going back to check on Ace."

"You're gonna let me win that easy?" I tease.

"You did not win. I forfeited. I need to check on Ace and make sure he has not slipped into a coma."

I watch Trisha swim away. The silver moon supplies enough light for me to track her to the shore.

Fine. I don't know where Trisha gets her elevated level of nurturing. We obviously do not share that similar bloodline.

It never mattered with Trisha if it was a stray dog, cat, or a bird with a broken wing. Growing up, she was always the one who had to take care of any animal in need. I just never thought she would feel the need to take care of wayward men, too.

To each their own, though.

I kick out of the treading water position and float on my back. The surf pulls and pushes me in a rhythmic trance. Even with my ears below the water, I hear the waves crashing louder and louder on the beach.

The vast silver moon shines down on me so bright and translucent I can see the pocks on its surface created long before humans inhabited the earth.

If I were a she-wolf, I would be changing about now. Or is the term a she-werewolf?

Random.

The odd thought of werewolves brings the topic of predators to mind. Predators and saltwater make me think about sharks. Specifically, great whites, which can eat me with one bite.

It's an excellent time to check on my friends and make sure

they are okay. I roll back onto my stomach and swim freestyle toward the shore. I strain for every bit of speed I can squeeze out of my stroke and kick. *Faster, I must go faster.* I swear I can feel the electrical energy of a great white right behind me.

I burrow my left hand into the sand. The surf crashes into my lower back as I stand, driving me to my knees. Great. Now I've got friction burns on my knees and sand in my panties.

Yeah, Ace was right. In the end, it's a sucky idea.

I back into the surf and try to get the sand out of my drawers with less than stellar results.

After my practice in futility, I trudge to our towels. "I'm coming over. You better have your shorts on, Ace."

"I see the shark didn't eat you," he says.

I plop down on my towel. "I'm too mean. I probably taste like a stinkbug."

I roll my head to the side as I hear Trisha snicker. She is trying to conceal her laughter. Ace looks thoroughly confused.

"It's not that funny, Trisha."

"You said it, not me."

I sit up and pull my T-shirt on. "I see your patient is still alive," I quip to Trisha.

"I told you earlier I feel better," Ace says.

"Your face begs to differ," I say.

"Are you going to press charges against Champ?" Trisha asks.

Ace's eyes open wider. "Why? So Champ can have a reason to tap dance on me again?"

"You need to let the police do their job," Trisha protests.

"Spoken like a true detective's daughter," I say.

"What is that supposed to mean?" Trisha raises her eyebrows.

"It's not like that, Trisha. It's just sometimes calling the police can just escalate something like this."

"Police are trained in these matters, April."

I start to explain myself to Trisha and then think better. I wouldn't be able to change her mind on this topic.

"Can we just change the subject?" Ace asks. "I had a fun time tonight, and I do not want to ruin it now."

"Besides getting your butt kicked," I tease.

He dips his chin and laughs. "Despite that."

Ace isn't so bad. Plus, he is pretty tough.

"What do you do up in Tennessee, Trisha?"

My cousin lights up at his interest. "Right now, I'm a paralegal. I'm working my way through law school—at night."

Ace rocks back on his elbows and looks genuinely impressed. "Well, I was right. I thought you were a smart chick."

"I don't know about all that," Trisha says.

"No, really. You must have a lot of ambition to do all that. I wish I had something I felt so passionate about."

"What do you like to do?" Trisha scoots closer to Ace.

"I don't know, that's just it." Ace picks up a handful of sand and allows it to sift through his fingers at the edge of our towels.

Their awkward conversation elicits a mental eye roll from me. It's like I magically popped into a junior high dance and am eavesdropping on two pubescent, hopeful future lovers. Burrowing my nose into the crook of my elbow, I cover my face with my arm. I make as if I'm taking a nap.

"There has to be something," Trisha coaxes.

"I like this. Hanging out with friends. I just don't really have any—well, maybe my roommate—before he started acting sketchy."

I can't resist. "Sketchy like drug lord, pimp, or maybe male escort?"

"Nah, nothing like that. At least, I don't think. Bart started dating this chick, and all of a sudden, he is quiet and weird around me."

"Sometimes, friends get distant when they start dating someone new. You should not take his mood change personally," Trisha says.

"Truth is, I kinda do take it personally. I overheard Bart say she is married. Maybe it is none of my business. Still, I told him he should knock it off. So, I stuck my nose in his business."

"That's not cool, Ace. If your buddy is dating a married woman, that is none of your beeswax unless he asks your opinion," I chime in. "If his moral compass is busted, you are not going to be able to fix it for him."

"What do you mean his moral compass is broken?" Trisha's hostile tone catches me off guard.

I lift my arm off my eyes and frown at her. "What? Do you think it's morally acceptable that his friend is dating a married woman? I doubt her husband will feel it's acceptable when he finds out."

"He might not find out," Trisha volleys back at me.

I raise up on one elbow. I'm not sure who jerked Trisha's chain, but she refuses to let the topic die. "Trisha, they always find out. Cheaters always think they are so discreet. Still, they always get caught. As they should."

"That's awfully close-minded of you, April. We do not know her situation. She might have a simply horrid husband who abuses her and maybe sees Ace's friend as a viable alternative to start a new life."

I don't understand what Trisha's hang-up is, but whenever she purses her lips like that, she's spoiling for a fight. I'm having too good of a time to argue. Besides, I do not know Ace's friend from Adam. "Yeah, you're probably right."

Trisha diverts her attention back to Ace. "Is he still sore about what you said?"

"No, I don't think so. But these long spells of not talking to each other are really creeping me out. It's almost like I no longer exist, or he wishes I would disappear."

"Maybe since he is spending more time with his girlfriend, he is too tired to talk."

"Too tired to say good morning? No, that's simply weird."

"That is weird," I agree with Ace.

Trisha glares at me. I shrug. "What? You don't think that is peculiar?"

"Maybe his roommate is going through a lot trying to figure things out. I'm sure it's confusing dating someone who is married. Especially if he really cares for them.

"Think of all the unknowns. Does she really love me, or is she just using me? What happens if her boyfriend finds out? Will he really leave his wife like he said he would?"

"Leave his wife?" I ask.

Trisha shudders. "I meant will she leave her husband."

Maybe there was more in Trisha's Shirley Temples than I tasted. "What is she like, Ace? Because right now, I'm imagining the Wicked Witch of the West. I do not want to be judgmental. Otherwise, Trisha might jump on me again. Please tell me she does have her reasons to cheat on her husband."

"I can't tell you. I've never met her."

I stare at Ace for a moment in hopes that he is kidding. Oh, no. That is not weird in the least. Most people have never met the girlfriend of their roommate and best friend—in another world.

How have their paths not met?

Since I have nothing else productive to add to their conversation, I lie down on my back, propping my hands behind my head. I stare up at the millions of silver pinpricks in the black velvet sky. The salt dries sticky on my skin as I listen to the crash of the surf. Can a girl get any luckier?

To think, a week ago, I was on the verge of homelessness. The idea of living in my Prius for six weeks had me highly concerned at the time.

Now my rent is paid through the summer, I have cash for the deposit on my Atlanta apartment, and a couple hundred dollars in reserves. And bonus, I'm marinating on the beach with no curfew, no schedule, and no care in the world. All compliments of a bit of lady luck at a Biloxi casino last week.

I need to soak it in while it lasts. My recruiting manager warned there would be long stretches of no vacations once I start at the firm. I will not settle for anything less than a partnership within five years. I know it's a big hairy goal, but I specialize in the near-impossible.

Yes, I'm sure a firm as elite as Master, Johnson, and Lloyd is full of talented attorneys. They are all pushing for the next available partnership. Still, they have not dealt with someone like me. April May Snow always plays to win, or I do not play at all.

I smile as I run the numbers through my head. It is difficult to decide between a high-rise condo in downtown Atlanta or a lake house in Buckhead. They both have their advantages. Sadly, I'll only be able to swing one before I make partner.

What? You must plan for success.

My mind wanders back to a simpler time when I developed my plan.

Trisha's family and mine went to the coast together each summer. One day I was sitting on a beach, not too far from here, and hatched the first plans of how I would escape Guntersville. It's been a long, hard road, but I have done it. I'm on the precipice of everything I ever imagined becoming a reality.

There were times when I had doubts. Times when I thought I had lost my faith. I even considered the goal might be too big for me a time or two. Still, I soldiered through. Now here I am—a winner—like I always planned.

Why would earning a partnership at the firm be any different?

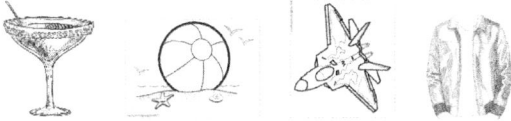

Chapter 4

"April, are you ready to go?"

Trisha is pushing my arm. I must have fallen asleep. "What time is it?"

"Almost three."

I scan left to right as I sit up. "Did Ace leave?"

"He got in the car. He said he was too cold."

"I guess that is one way of making sure we give him a ride back to his car," I say as I stand and pull my shorts on.

"To his apartment. He didn't drive," Trisha corrects me.

"He doesn't have a car?"

Trisha frowns until her lips become a thin line. "I'm sure he does. It's not unusual for people to get rides when they go to a bar."

I flip my towel into the air shaking out the sand. "Whatever. But let's get home. I'm beat."

I see Ace snoozing in the passenger seat as we approach the car. Trisha and I stow our gear in the trunk of her dad's car, and I get into the back seat behind her.

Ace stirs when we shut the door. "Oh, hey. Do you want to get up front, April?"

"No. It's easier to whack you on the back of the head from back here."

Ace nods his head slowly. "Good to know."

Trisha starts the car. "It's hard to believe she won miss con-geniality at her high school's beauty pageant her senior year."

I stretch out my long legs. "That is a lie, Ace. Do not believe her."

"True story," Trisha insists. "What is your apartment address on North Davies, Ace?"

I run my fingers through my hair. "North Davies? Darn, Ace. You are halfway to Montgomery."

"Don't pay her any attention, Ace. She gets grouchy when she's tired."

Ace glances at me before answering Trisha, "Thirty-nine twenty-seven. I appreciate you giving me a ride."

"Don't even mention it," Trisha says.

I do not like to admit it—most likely because Trisha is so good at nurturing, and I bite at it—still, giving Ace a ride home is the least we can do. I did incapacitate him with an elbow to the ster-num moments before a WWE look-alike decided to tap dance on his ribs. The fact he stuck with us after all that earns the boy a ride home.

The vibration of our car has about put me back to sleep as we pull into the parking lot of a seedy-looking apartment complex. I suppose it's hard to afford anything much better on a floor cleaner's salary, even with a roommate.

Seeing Ace's living conditions makes me feel about six inches tall. Sometimes I forget how fortunate I am that my parents paid for my living expenses for the last seven years. I found out last week just how difficult it is to make your rent.

"Mi castillo," Ace says as Trisha stops the car. "Thank you again for the ride. I hope I did not put you too far from your place."

"Glad to see you get home safe, Ace," Trisha says.

I exit the car and wait at the passenger door as Ace gets out. "Are you sure you are okay?" I ask him.

"Right as rain," he says with a grin. "I appreciate you letting me tag along. I had a fun time."

I have no idea what comes over me. I step forward and pull

Ace into a hug. I pat him awkwardly on the shoulder, as I'm not a hugger by nature. "Alright, be good."

Ace chuckles. "You too."

I yell at his back as he unlocks his front door, "And stay out of the way of your moody roommate."

He gives us a thumbs up and disappears into his apartment.

I shut the car door. "Okay, spill the beans."

"About what?" Trisha starts the car.

"I know that was some Freudian slip earlier. It's the only thing that explains why you were so irritated we judged Ace's room-mate harshly for dating a married woman."

Trisha cuts her eyes in my direction. "I have no idea *what* you are talking about."

Now would be an excellent time for me to use my psychic powers and glean the information I want from Trisha rather than being forced to pump her with questions the whole drive home. Except she is family.

No. I don't have some sort of privacy code barring me from using my psychic abilities on the family. Believe me, if I thought it would work, I would grab Trisha's arm right now. Reading her thoughts without her permission would be an intrusion of her privacy. Still, my hyperactive curiosity often overrides trivial things like other people's right to privacy.

Unfortunately, my "gifts" doesn't work with people I have had long relationships with. At least not always. It's random.

If we are both highly emotional, there is a chance I might catch her thoughts for a second. But not likely.

Besides, Trisha has a good heart.

My "gifts" flips on the fastest when I'm around people I have never met. Especially folks who are up to no good. My powers come alive when I am around people with dark, evil cores.

I will have to get the story out of her the old-fashioned way. Play on her conscience. "So, it's going to be like that?"

"What?" Trisha asks.

"You are going to shut out your cousin. The one person who really understands you. You will feel better if you share the burden."

"I doubt that."

This must be a particularly juicy personal confession. Trisha usually gives in to me quickly.

"Come on. You know I would tell you."

She snorts. "Yeah, right. There are CIA operatives with fewer secrets than you."

Fair. "That is not true."

We ride in silence as my brain spins at a feverish speed. I imagine all manner of lurid secrets she may be withholding. I finally rationalize that Trisha simply made a slip of the tongue when she says, "He will leave his wife."

It's none of my business. I'll let Trisha have her secret. No matter how agitated and unsatisfied her mystery leaves me.

"Where did you meet him?" I can't help myself.

"Who?"

"Your married lover."

"What!" Trisha's jaw drops. "Where did that come from, April? You are so completely off-base with that assumption. I cannot believe you have the nerve to suggest that."

Daddy always says the hit dog yells the loudest.

"You little hussy." I grin.

"No. April, no. You are wrong."

I turn in my seat to face her. "I am right. Wow, how crazy is this? Our own little Trisha is a charlatan."

Her eyes narrow. "It is not like that at all."

"Okay, then explain."

"No, you wouldn't understand."

"You're probably right. Relationships are tough enough without complicating it by dating a man who has already done the 'for better or worse' with a woman and not signed divorce papers yet."

"We are not dating!"

"Hooking up or whatever you want to call it," I joke.

The tensing muscles running up Trisha's neck show prominently. I have overstepped my boundaries. She is angry.

"It is not like that. He does not even know I have these feelings for him," she grumbles.

Her confession is not the one I expected, and it knocks me off-center. "I don't understand, Trisha."

"Of course, you don't!" she snaps. "Every man you come in contact with notices you and wants you. If a guy notices me, do you know what they want? Me to get them a cup of coffee or a deli sandwich, depending on the time of day."

"They say food is the way to a man's heart." I try to make light of her self-deprecating comment.

"I'm serious here, and you are making jokes?"

Trisha's temper rarely flares. Seeing her so upset pains me. "I'm serious, too, Trisha. You have the most beautiful eyes and a sexy body. Most importantly, you are the nicest, most caring person I know. You are the sweet Hallmark Christmas special heroine with a killer NC-17 figure. You don't even know it."

She huffs. "You are so full of it, April May."

"No, I'm not. I'm telling you the truth, Trisha. Your Mr. Married Guy does not notice you because he is *married* and in love with his wife. I predict quite happily. Am I right?"

She exhales. "Yes. She is beautiful, nice, and insanely perfect."

"See, that is you in a few years. You will find Mr. Lightning Bolt to Your Heart, and you two will be the perfect couple. You just have not found each other yet."

"This sounds like another one of your sermons of bull. Should I put on a pair of waders?"

"No bull. Just the facts, Trisha."

Her expression softens. "Do you really think it's possible?"

"I know so."

It is a fact. It is also factual that Prince Charming would have already found her if Trisha would put a little more effort into the "wrapping." Unfortunately for the prince, Trisha disguises herself in the dowdiest clothes ever worn by a woman under thirty. Not to mention—except when I'm with her—she is a homebody who prefers spending the evening either studying, reading romances, or playing cards with her dad.

She cannot remain invisible forever. One day some great guy will see her shine through her matronly façade. Then it will be one of those sappy, ridiculously implausible romantic comedies she so enjoys.

That makes me happy for her. I desperately want a romance fairytale to come true for her. She is tailor-made for a happily ever after.

Me? Not so much. I'm a little concerned about myself lately.

Despite all the enjoyment I get from hanging out with men and my sincere appreciation for most things masculine. It has been a long time since a guy has set my motor running. To Trisha's point, I have had many opportunities.

I think my starter might be broken.

Until a few weeks ago, I have been too busy with graduation and securing suitable employment to concern myself with my nonexistent love life. More recently, I have been solely focused on making enough money to survive the summer. Consequently, I have not given sex, let alone romance, any thought.

"Do you think he is okay? It really bothers me that he would not let us take him to the hospital," Trisha says.

"Ace?"

"Yes. Those bruises look bad."

"Oh, they are not done yet. I'm sure he will have raccoon eyes in the morning."

"Should we have left him alone? I mean with the concussion and everything."

I shake my head. "I have seen concussed before. He seemed okay once he came to. I believe he is a lot tougher than he looks."

Trisha giggles. "He was dressed as a pilot, and he didn't look tough to you?"

I click my tongue. "If you thought he was a pilot, I have a few other things I would like to sell you."

"He wasn't bad looking," Trisha objects.

"Trisha Hirsh, are you sweet on him?"

"Lord, no." She holds her mouth open in mock horror. "What gave you that idea?"

"I don't know. I suppose the way you fawned over him?"

"I did not."

"April, get him a beer," I mock.

"You almost killed him. The poor guy nearly asphyxiated."

She did have to bring that up. It sort of takes the fun out of mocking her reaction. "I'm confused. You really didn't like him?"

"Not like that. I was just worried about Ace. I thought you were the one who liked him."

I start laughing. I stop as I realize Trisha is sincere. "Why would you think that? You just got done saying I about killed him."

Trisha's eyebrows shoot up. "Seriously? Do I really have to bring up Tommy Baron?"

"Now that is not fair, Trisha. What was that, like third grade?"

"Seventh. Tommy was petrified that if he did not stay your boyfriend, you were going to beat him up."

"I do not know where he would have gotten that idea." Although I might have mentioned it to him once or twice in a not-so-veiled threat. All the other girls in our class had boyfriends, and Tommy Baron was the only boy not taken. I was not about to be the only girl not partnered up when the music stopped in the mean girls' game of musical boyfriends. It reminds me how much easier life was when I was bigger, faster, and stronger than most boys my age.

"He moved to Nashville a couple of years ago."

I'm surprised Trisha kept up with him. "Did he decide he wanted to be a country music star?" I tease.

"No. He is doing something in real estate. He came into our law office a few months back," Trisha says.

The pieces of the puzzle begin to fall into place for me. "Who did he marry?"

"I don't think he is married," she says.

I was so close. I just knew Tommy Baron was the married man Trisha has a crush on. Great, now my mind is spinning in circles again, and it had quieted for a moment.

Chapter 5

Trisha turns into our condominium parking lot and turns off the car. "I wish we had gotten Ace's number. I would feel better if we could call and check in on him," she says.

"I'm sure he is already asleep by now," I say as we walk up the sidewalk.

Trisha unlocks the front door to the condominium. The scent of bacon wafts onto the front porch. Despite having eaten only a few hours earlier, my stomach grumbles. "Is your dad cooking?"

"I hope so. Otherwise, the condo is on fire."

We toss our purses on the foyer table as we make our way into the kitchen. Norman is perched on a high-back stool, nursing a cup of coffee. If not for a tiny splinter of bacon on his plate, I would believe he had just now pulled the red flatware out of the cupboard.

"Look what the cat drug in," he says with a knowing grin.

"I thought you said you were spending the night at your friend's?" Trisha says.

Norman cranes his neck to look toward the front door. "Do you two have boys with you or something?"

"*No.* What gave you that idea?" Trisha asks.

He chuckles. "I don't know. You sound sort of disappointed I'm here. I thought I might be cramping your style."

"As if."

"Are you girls hungry?"

"I'm good," I lie. My stomach is still highly disappointed there is not a heaping pile of bacon to devour.

Norman slides off his high-backed stool. "It wouldn't be anything to cook you a couple of pancakes. I have some batter mix left. I will have to throw it out otherwise."

"Well, we wouldn't want you to have to waste it," I say.

"I guess I'll take a small one," Trisha says.

Norman turns on the gas stove. "What are you two doing roaming around this late anyway? Only animals and professional ballplayers stay out this late."

"Lord, you sound like my daddy now," I grumble.

"Well—and ladies of ill repute," he continues to tease. "But I know you two had a proper upbringing. So, you wouldn't be doing anything illegal."

"April almost killed a guy tonight. But then she saved him," Trisha blurts.

I didn't tell Trisha I wanted to keep the Ace story between us. Still, I assumed what happens during girls' night stays amongst the girls.

But, my bad. I forget Trisha is an open book.

"It sounds to me like you broke even with the law on that one." Norman focuses on the Teflon-coated skillet in his hand too much to sell his nonchalant tone.

Trisha and I sit down on the high-backed stools. "He deserved it. He was imitating a Blue Angel," I explain.

"*No.* I can't believe anybody at a bar late at night in Pensacola would be lying about their profession."

I roll my eyes at my uncle's sarcasm. I would return fire, but the pancakes look delicious. I don't want to push my luck.

"I suspect that is a pretty common game around here," he continues.

"Speaking of games—how did your card game go tonight?" Trisha asks.

"I broke even on purpose. We are here for another week, and I would like to be invited back for another game or two. I will wipe the boys out on our last night."

You do not want to play cards against my uncle. Numbers have a particular stickiness in his mind. Norman can run complex math problems in his head. When it comes to card games, he excels at counting cards even when not trying.

I watch Trisha and her dad interact as she fills him in on all the details of our evening, including the points I wish she would keep between us. But I also understand her desire to share everything with him is born out of necessity.

Trisha and Norman have been climbing out of their grief for Aunt Nancy for twelve years. My aunt died from breast cancer at the way-too-early age of forty-four. She spent the last year and half of her brief life fighting bravely against the disease, as everyone likes to recount.

Call me a sore loser, but I'm not one to get a spirit lift out of the whole "good fight" award. I watched my aunt weather increasingly larger doses of chemotherapy in hopes of staving off death. At the same time, the disease ravaged her beautiful body and suffocated her infectious optimism. It was a Pyrrhic victory, sans the victory.

Sorry. I'm still salty over my aunt being stolen from me. I'm not sure I have dealt with the loss.

There was a time when the entire family was concerned Norman might not pull out of his depression. It was universe-altering when he, a man built for marriage, lost his life partner. He fell utterly silent, lost over seventy pounds, and his hair turned gunmetal grey overnight.

There was talk Trisha might come live with my family at the lake. Selfishly, I was thrilled at the proposition. There is a dearth of young females on my side of the family.

Still, I knew deep down inside that Trisha needed her dad more. She needed to stay with her remaining parent and the most vital link to her lost mother. They were on a journey together. The rest of us could only watch.

It was not counseling, pills, or time that pulled Norman back from the brink of extinction. It was Trisha.

Trisha pried the man open like a small stream exerting its continual friction against a stone. Consistent and unrelenting force always wins regardless of the hardness of the stone. Trisha is persistence and patience personified.

As I polish my plate with a hot, buttered piece of toast Norman pulled from the oven, he tosses the last remnants of his coffee into the sink and rinses the pot. "You girls don't worry about cleaning the kitchen. I will finish up after I catch some shut-eye."

"Are you going to the beach with us in the morning, Dad?" Trisha asks.

He laughs. "I will do the tourists a favor and not expose all this manliness on the beach." He pats his belly.

"If you change your mind, I'm setting my alarm for eight."

"Thank you for the offer, but I'm meeting some of the guys for lunch at Joe Patti's. I can almost taste that fried seafood sampler now." He folds a dishtowel over the oven handle and walks out of the kitchen.

"I wish he would start eating better," Trisha says when Norman is out of earshot.

"I think he looks great for a man approaching sixty."

"I'm not worried about his physique. I'm worried about how clogged the inside of his arteries looks."

I begin to argue that one of the rewards of surviving until you are sixty should be you can do whatever you want. It is not like Norman is putting as many years of life at risk if he decides to eat a pound of bacon and become an avid skydiver.

If he had a young family, well, that would be irresponsible.

In Norman's case? Let the man live. By Trisha's jerky movement and clipped tone, I can tell I would be wasting my breath. So, I keep the thought to myself.

"Are you sure you want to get up at eight?" I take a quick look at my phone. "That is only four hours away."

"I want to make certain we get a good spot on the beach. I plan to sleep most of the day anyway."

That sounds like an excellent plan. Trisha is clever like that.

The condo is a three-bedroom with three and a half baths. The full baths are ensuite to the rooms. Trisha's room has two full-size beds. Even though my toiletries are in the bathroom down the hall, I end up sleeping in her room. I guess "spend the night" habits die hard.

The slight clacking of the paddle fan is putting me to sleep. I hear Trisha whisper, but I can't understand her. Pardon?"

"It's my boss," she says slightly louder.

I stare into the darkness. "What about your boss?"

"The guy I was talking about. It is the law firm partner I work for—Austin."

I consider the implications. All the bad tropes from B-list movies come to mind, and I cringe. "But he does not know how you feel, right?"

"No. He is oblivious to me. Other than what I can do for him at work."

Thank the Lord for small favors. I can only hope she keeps it that way. It would be terrible if she put herself through the embarrassment of being rejected—and eventually with her conscience, the guilt if she pursued her feelings.

I don't have any words of encouragement or advice for her current plight. I consider telling her she needs to knock it off and bury her feelings. That would only agitate her. Trisha is smart enough to realize acting on her desires would be a catastrophe. That is why she hasn't—yet.

I stare into the dark, listen to the fan, and hope she stays sane while never giving in to her passion for the man.

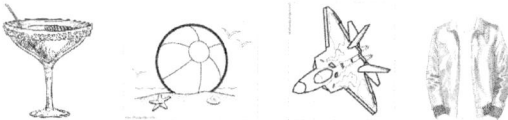

Chapter 6

Trisha insists we set up the beach tent. I complain the entire time since it seems so unnecessary.

My whining is induced in part from sleep deprivation and part hangover. I'm not ashamed to admit when my self-discipline has failed me.

We finish the tent a little bit before nine.

Sometime later, something wakes me, and I squint against the sun. Having reached the sky's apex, it must be around noon.

Trisha was right about the tent. We have been able to nap comfortably in the shade off and on for three hours. The sand under my oversized beach towel forms perfectly to my body as the breeze lightly tickles my skin. The crash of the tide begins to lull me back to sleep.

Suddenly, I realize I'm parched. I look up and find the cooler we rolled onto the beach is more than an arm's length away. Considering it would require me to get up. It looks like it is a long way off. I weigh just how thirsty I am.

My mouth is too dry to finish the process when I attempt to swallow. I grunt in frustration and pull myself up onto all fours.

Once I retrieve an ice-cold water from the cooler, I try out one of the low-slung beach chairs we lugged onto the beach. This, too, at Trisha's insistence. I settle onto the canvas seat. I open the top of my water and reposition my sunglasses squarely on my nose.

Wow. I watch as an attractive couple, about college age, crosses in front of me, holding hands. My mind spins stories about them.

She is a business major who hopes to go into advertising. He is on a tennis scholarship at UAB. That is not fiction or psychic reading. It is clearly printed on his Kelly green, clingy wet T-shirt, *UAB Tennis.*

I suck down half my bottle of water. People-watching is by far my favorite activity.

"What time is it?"

I cut my eyes to Trisha, who has not moved. "Almost noon. Why? Are you hungry?"

"After back-to-back breakfasts this morning, I would not think it possible. But maybe we should get something to eat in an hour."

There is no arguing with that. Especially for me. I can eat at any time.

"Wake me up in half an hour," Trisha mumbles. Her cheek is pressed against her towel.

"Okay."

I consider breaking out my phone to read a story or scan social media. Why would I do that, though? The view is outstanding. Plus, there are hundreds of interesting people passing in front of me.

It does surprise me that Trisha has not mentioned our buddy Ace since we made it to the beach. I expected we might be forced to make a wellness call to his apartment sometime today to put her conscience at ease. But nope. She has not brought his name up once. I guess she is already over his crisis.

I'm just now beginning to deal with the events of last night. I'm often afflicted with delayed reactions to crises. The half-full water bottle in my hand trembles.

The level of violence Champ doled out in a few brief seconds on Ace is hard to fathom. I have no doubt if I had not intervened, Champ would be in jail this morning for murder and Ace would be at the coroner's office.

Why me? Why did I have to be the one to intervene? I had no business going up against Champ.

My face is still sore where he backhanded me. I'm fortunate he caught me mainly under the chin. The bruise will not be readily seen.

"When we go for lunch. I want to go by Ace's and check in on him," Trisha says.

That is delayed concern from Trisha. She must finally be working those Shirley Temples out of her bloodstream.

"Okay," I say.

I return my attention to the beach and watch a trio of sandpipers chase the tide in and out. They stab at the sand hundreds of times, extracting tiny clams from the crystal white sand.

I will never carry a gun again. It may not be a rational decision. Especially since it saved Ace's life last night and kept Champ from serving a life sentence without parole. Still, I did something last night I never thought I would do. I pointed a loaded weapon at a man and was forced to consider squeezing the trigger.

How fundamentally altered would my life be if I tightened my right pointer finger last night and squeezed off a round? Even if justified, I would never forgive myself if I killed Champ.

It seems odd to be having this line of thought. I'm by no means a gun fanatic. Still, I have been around firearms all my life. They have never bothered me before now.

Things changed for me in Biloxi. I had never witnessed firsthand any gun violence before last week. I'm sure seeing the carnage created by a crazed man directing fire at innocence significantly impacts my current psyche.

That's fair. Probably an understatement.

Two highly tanned guys are blocking my view of my sandpipers and ocean now. The shorter of the two, with an exceptionally muscle-toned physique, is talking to his taller partner. The taller man has come to a stop and is peering under our tent. He is not paying any attention to what his shorter, "Greek god" friend says.

Is he leering at me? No. His eyes are a little to the—my word, he is practically staring a hole in Trisha's bikini bottoms.

"Would you like to borrow my phone to take a picture?" I yell at him. "It has an excellent zoom lens if you need it."

Tall Guy's eyes open wide with alarm before he looks down at the sand. His tan is so dark, I would never be able to see if he is blushing. Still, I suspect his heart rate just shot through the roof. *Good.*

Greek God turns his attention to me. After a moment, he appears to comprehend what took place.

He punches his buddy hard on the arm and starts toward our tent. Precisely what I do not want.

"Please let me apologize for my friend's rudeness. He was raised by wolves."

Greek God is a man obviously used to turning on his charm to get out of uncomfortable situations. I do not typically care for men like him. My face betrays me as I smile.

Trisha rolls to her side. Shielding her eyes with her hand, she looks up at our visitor. "Hi."

Seeing easier entry into our good graces, Greek God squats and extends his hand to Trisha. "Hi. I'm Wesley Greenwood." He gestures with his thumb over his shoulder. "And this is my buddy, Hank Knox."

Trisha sits up. Tucking her legs under her, she shakes Wesley's hand. "Hi, Wesley. Are you a friend of April's?"

Wesley flashes a bedazzling smile. "Not yet. But I plan to be."

Trisha favors me a questioning look. I clear the situation up for her. "Wesley is chatting us up because of his guilty-looking buddy." I point at his friend. "Hank, is it"—Hank gives a guilty nod, and I continue—"was ogling your knickers."

Trisha pulls her beach towel up, covering her legs and waist. I doubt she realizes she did that.

"Actually, I'm chatting you up—as you say—because you ladies are the most beautiful women we have seen today. I thought it would be interesting to explore if your personalities are equally enchanting."

Before today I was positive I had heard every cheesy pickup line in the world. Then Wesley tries one on me I never heard before. The disturbing thing is, rather than his weak line aggravating me, my tummy does a tiny flip. Totally inappropriate.

"I hate to disappoint you then," I say.

Wesley unleashes an uber-sexy smile. "Then don't."

It is two short, itty-bitty words. Somehow, Wesley makes it sound—and, more irritatingly, feel—like a sexual proposition. My feminist sensibilities yell, "Jerk!" My body is asking, "Can I touch—please?"

"Hi, I'm Hank." Hank extends his hand to me. Reluctantly I shake hands. He turns and shakes Trisha's hand.

"You know I was just telling Hank about a place on Navarre Beach the locals insist has the best fish tacos on the panhandle," Wesley says.

"Was this while he was ogling my cousin?"

Hank crosses his chest with his arms. "I'm really sorry about that. I'm not like that. My mind checked out on me."

"Apology accepted," Trisha interjects. "I know people probably think I'm crazy at times because I will be thinking about something, and I might be staring at the wall or just up into the sky. I won't even be aware of what I'm looking at."

Yeah, that is not what was going on. I'm sure Hank was aware he was staring at Trisha's vajayjay.

"Like I was saying. I told Hank we ought to check out this restaurant for lunch. But since we have the good fortune of meeting you two, perhaps you would like to come with us."

"That's sweet of you. Trisha and I had a huge breakfast."

"What are you talking about? We just said we were going to leave for lunch," Trisha says.

Wesley once again takes the easier path and ignores me. "Perfect. It's settled then."

I give Trisha my meanest stink-eye. She simply ignores me.

"Do you want to follow us in your car, or do you want to ride with us?" Wesley asks.

"We can ride with you," Trisha says.

Right, and I'm expecting them to be driving a VW Bug like Ted Bundy. I crush the empty water bottle in my hand loudly. The noise gets Trisha's attention. When she looks at my face, I imagine she remembers all the nights we stayed up watching horror documentaries we had no business watching. She comes to her "stranger danger" senses belatedly.

"Actually, we have a bit of a tight schedule. Why don't you give us the address, and we will meet you there?"

Wesley turns to me. "What is your cell number? I'll text you their address and website."

As I recite my cell phone number to Wesley, I feel like I have an out-of-body experience. There is no way I am giving my actual phone number to a guy I just met on the beach. Trisha's bad judgment must be contagious.

My cell phone rings. I do a double-take of Wesley's hands as I try to figure out how he can text me the information that quickly.

My brain kicks into gear. I realize it is just a coincidence. Looking at the caller ID, I see it's my uncle calling.

"Are your arteries permanently clogged from all that fried food?" I joke as I answer the phone.

"Where are you, April?"

Something in his tone cuts my humor short. "On the beach with Trisha. Why?"

"I need you two back at the condo immediately."

Every muscle in my body tightens. "Is everything all right?"

"I'm not sure yet. We'll see. Promise me you will hurry."

"Yes, sir. We will."

I disconnect the line and stare at my phone. I'm running every scenario I can think of through my mind and can't come up with a single reason Norman would be calling us back to the condo.

"What is the matter? Is he okay?" Trisha stands and looks at my phone as if it will give her a clue about what her dad said.

"Your dad is fine," I reassure her.

Wesley opens his hands, palms up. "If you ladies need to take a raincheck on the lunch, we totally understand."

Wesley and Hank help us break down the tent and carry our gear to our car. Under different circumstances, I would be concerned about Wesley and Hank knowing the make and model of Trisha's car and her license plate number.

I'm a lot more cynical these days. Sue me. I'm lucky I do not have a diagnosable case of paranoia after the events of the last few weeks.

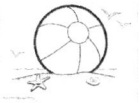

Chapter 7

Trisha drives at her usual infuriatingly slow pace. Despite the fact her dad said to get to the condo as quickly as possible.

I do not ask her to speed up the pace. Something in my gut tells me whatever Norman wants to discuss with us, I'm not going to enjoy it.

The two police cars sitting at the curb confirm my gut feeling as we drive into the parking lot. I know Norman has a fair number of contacts at the police department, but I doubt any of them would drive marked police cruisers to pay him a visit. His friends are more of the unmarked detective's vehicle type.

"I thought you said he was okay," Trisha says with alarm in her tone.

"I'm sure he is fine."

"Then why are the police here for him?"

Trisha is obviously a little slow on the come. "I think it has nothing to do with your dad and everything to do with the altercation at the bar last night."

She parks the car. "That is stupid. We didn't start that. The big dude did."

I quickly see the error of my ways. Last night I thought it best for us to clear out of the bar and act like nothing happened. In retrospect, I created the opportunity for Champ to file a complaint and control the narrative with the police.

I berate myself as we walk to the front door. I'm obviously not near as good of a defense attorney as I like to think I am. Still, this will be a lesson I will carry with me when I defend my clients in the future.

I open the door. Norman and two uniformed police officers turn toward me. I'm not expecting them to be just inside the door. My spine stiffens, causing me to draw back in surprise.

There are deep creases in my uncle's face as he says, "See, officers. No one is avoiding you."

"Hi. What's the trouble?" I try to act nonchalant. I hope they do not notice I'm shaking like a loose leaf in a tornado.

"April Snow?" The broader of the two officers steps closer to me as he asks.

"That's me. What is this about, officer?"

"Were you at Three Sheets to the Wind bar last night?"

My suspicions are confirmed. I feel a slight case of nausea coming on as I know this may not end well. "Yes, sir."

"We have reports you were involved in an altercation last night at the bar."

I'm not positive if he is asking a question or stating a fact. I answer anyway. "I was not involved by choice. But after my friend was beaten unconscious and I was backhanded, I suppose I became involved."

The police officer's stare is unyielding. His gold-brown eyes bore into me as if he could read my mind. "We also have a report that you pulled a gun on one of the patrons."

"Pulled a gun on the assailant would be more accurate," I say.

The officer continues to study me. I'm sure he hopes to see beads of perspiration break out on my forehead, or my eyes begin to jerk to the left. Still, I did nothing wrong. I have nothing to be nervous about. At least, that is what I keep repeating in my mind.

"Do you still have the gun in your possession?"

That's a stupid question. Of course, I do. "Yes." I move toward my purse, which I left on the foyer table since I chose to only carry my keys and wallet to the beach.

Dang it. I stop in midstride.

"What's the trouble, Miss Snow?" the officer asks.

I know he does not mean to, but his voice sounds condescending. I turn to Trisha and hold out my hand. "I need your keys."

Trisha looks confused but hands me her keys. I make for the front door, and both officers follow me only steps behind.

It is bad enough that I pulled a gun with good cause last night on Champ. The police are really not going to like the fact I left a loaded gun in the car's glove compartment.

Yes, I know. Guns stolen from vehicles are a significant source of illegal weapons on the street. I was tired last night. It slipped my mind.

My world spends out of control as I open the glove compartment. It is empty except for service records and a few spare napkins saved from fast food meals.

I pull the maintenance record logbook and the napkins out of the glove compartment until nothing remains inside. The gun had been on top of everything, with no good reason to be below the napkins and logbook.

I stare at the pile of papers on the passenger seat as the reality of the situation settles in on me. *I am so screwed.*

"You do have your gun. Don't you, Miss Snow?"

I do not respond to the officer's question. I should not say anything else and ask for a lawyer. The officers know something they are not sharing with me. Something that will really ruin my week. If not my life.

Where is my stupid gun?

"You might want to check under the seat, too. Those Bond Arms Backups are so small they can disappear very easily. I'm not fond of two-shot pistols, but the forty-five ACP is great when you are up close and personal."

Mystery number one is solved. I now know where my gun is, and my gut clenches severely.

Mystery number two, how did these friendly police officers get my gun? Something tells me I'm not going to like the answer to mystery number two.

I turn to face the police officer. I attempt to relax and put on my best poker face. If I have learned anything about a question-and-answer session, he who provides the most information loses. My plan is to remain silent as much as possible and still be "cooperative."

The officer's eyes narrow. "The gun, ma'am."

"I don't have it."

"Where is it?"

"I don't know." And that is the truth.

The officer continues to study me. I fight to keep my heart rate down as his intense glare drives up my anxiety level.

Where did I put that stupid gun? The last time I remember seeing it. I dropped it into the glove compartment so I could go swimming.

No, I put it there to separate myself from it.

Typically, I would place it back into my purse where it belongs. But the situation in the bar had discombobulated me.

When I reached the car. I concluded carrying a firearm is more trouble than it is worth. I decided I did not want to bother with a gun anymore.

That is how it ended up in the glove compartment. How it ended up out of the glove compartment is now the prize-winning question.

Sure, I had a good bit to drink last night. Still, I was stone-cold sober when we made it home. I do not remember sliding my weapon back into my purse when we finished our swim. Even if I had, my purse has been in the apartment all day.

"Are you sure you do not know where your gun is?"

"Positive," I say.

The officer's eyes open wider as the right side of his mouth flexes up briefly.

"But if I had to guess. My money is on *you* knowing exactly where it is," I say.

His eyebrows raise briefly. "Miss Snow, we would appreciate you accompanying us to the station so we can sort this out."

Sort what out? Okay, so my gun is missing. I admit that is not particularly responsible of me. But it is not like I killed someone.

If these turkeys were around last night. Or if the massive waste of masculine flesh at Three Sheets to the Wind—their security guard—had done his job. I would not have needed to draw my gun. But they were not, he did not, and I had to stop Champ from murdering Ace.

This is so not fair!

"Officers, is that necessary? I would be more than happy to brew you a cup of coffee and give you privacy in the kitchen," Norman suggests.

"Sorry, sir. We were given explicit instructions to bring her to the station if we located her before the detectives."

My mind races to two weeks back. A foreboding sense of déjà vu disrupts my poker face. This is a repeat of the situation I struggled through after my friend's girlfriend was murdered. Initially, I was a person of interest in her case.

I begin to pant as anxiety builds in me. "You can at least tell me what this is all about."

The officer frowns. "I would think that would be obvious. Your missing firearm, of course."

"What about it?" My voice sounds high-pitched and tinny.

The stout officer's expression hardens again. "I'm not at liberty to say." He gestures toward the front door. "Please come along now. Perhaps we can figure this out together."

It is a standard request. I'm sure he has used it at least a hundred times. That is why his request sounds so non-adversarial. The word "together" stokes hope in my heart. A fool's hope.

I shake off the hypnosis of his request and plead to my uncle, "Norman."

His forehead is lined heavily with concern. "Go with them for now, April. I will be right behind you, and I will give Howard a call. He will know what to do."

My uncle Howard is a defense attorney genius. His talent is wasted practicing in our small hometown of Guntersville. Still, he will not be able to do much from five hours away. Maybe he knows someone locally who can help me.

I resign myself to my current plight. No pleading my innocence will help. Besides, I do not even know what to claim I am innocent of yet.

The officer helps me into the back of the cruiser. I'm not wearing any fashion faux pas stainless steel bracelets, on the positive side of things.

As the cruiser takes off, the officer does not turn the flashing lights on to notify the neighbors to look at the criminal in the back seat of the green and white cop car. I do appreciate that gesture of civility.

I lean forward, not wanting to sit back against the vinyl seat that reeks of a suffocating mixture of urine and bleach. I already feel filthy and violated. Not to mention I am scared and angry.

I close my eyes in defeat and ponder all the spectacular ways my life bites. No, I am not being melodramatic. My life has been one complete suckfest the last month. I can smile and be positive while working through this patch of rotten luck. Still, it is insanity not to be honest with myself and call it like it is. To put a positive spin on all this crazy is, well, crazy.

It is equivalent to enjoying a bowl of ice cream in a burning house. Sure, I can say the ice cream is tasty. I'm thankful to be enjoying a bowl of ice cream—but I'm in a burning house!

My life is a raging dumpster fire.

I could live with all the trouble if I were shady or had not been mindful to live my life right. Not just improving myself with higher education. I have been attempting to live a more responsible life and force myself to pay attention to other people's needs.

No, I'm not perfect. I realize I am a work in progress. Still, I'm a good person. So why are all these awful things happening to me in rapid-fire succession lately?

As if I do not know. I'm conveniently ignoring the white elephant in what is my life.

During the seven years in Tuscaloosa, my psychic abilities waned and atrophied. By the end of the fall semester of my freshman year, I all but quit receiving psychic vibes from other students.

The only ghost sightings I had were the spirits that unfortunately resided at my sorority. Voices in my mind were scarce, and only when my mental partition faltered. Except for a few exceptions, I had no paranormal incidents.

I actually came to believe—or at least hope—I phased out of the psychic stage of my life. As if it were only an awkward period. Like when I was twelve, I grew a full eighteen inches taller overnight and remained the same weight. Or at least it seemed like overnight...

Let me tell you, it is not easy to blend in with your friends and not be called hurtful names when you resemble a baby giraffe.

Of course, I totally ignored the warnings of both Granny and Nana on the subject. Both grandmothers cautioned me I should expect my "gifts"—as they like to refer to it. I feel "private nightmare" is more apropos—increasing strength with age. Once again, they were right.

What I cannot figure out is, why so suddenly? It is not like I aged overnight. I would have expected a more gradual increase. Plus, why did the psychic ability stay dormant for seven years?

I have so many questions and so few answers. The only person I can blame is me. I refused to listen to or seek the counsel of my grandmothers. I chose to simply avoid the topic. Now I can see my skirting the issue was a dreadful mistake.

I'm sure an average person—that is, most people outside of my family—would explain the wild and dangerous things that happened to me as coincidence. They were merely a run of bad luck.

I know in my bones that is dead wrong.

It is no coincidence the unfortunate events began shortly after a psychic episode. The supernatural events seem to be like a set of colossal gears in my brain slipping into motion, shaking the equilibrium of my brain. Somehow the vibration of that slippage in my mind magnetizes evil and pulls it to me.

I fold in half, crossing my arms under my knees and burying my face against my jeans. I am fricking driving myself crazy.

Magnetizing myself and attracting evil? Nobody has ever mentioned that to me. Where in the world did that come from?

Opposites attract, April.

The thought has such clarity, I am not sure if it is inside or outside my head. Chill bumps run up my spine.

I hope the little voice is off the mark. Otherwise, I am in way over my head.

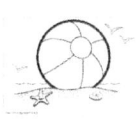

Chapter 8

The police cruiser comes to a stop. The stouter of the two officers—his badge reads Lancaster—opens the door for me.

"We will try to wrap this up as quickly as possible, so you can
get back to your family."

I take note of the sun just a few degrees past high noon. Given
my present gallows attitude, I speculate I will be looking at a full
moon the next time I breathe fresh air.

The exterior of the police station is a 1960s utilitarian block
building with a fancy stucco façade in desperate need of pressure washing and trim painting. The station's interior surprises
me as the marble floor is buffed to a mirror shine. The cubicle
walls look well taken care of, if not new.

I follow Officer Lancaster to the second door on the left. He
opens the door and motions for me to enter. "Would you like
coffee, Coke, or water?"

The stern-guy stare is gone, replaced by kinder eyes. "No. But
thank you for asking."

"Okay. Just have a seat, and Detective Keaton will be in
shortly."

The door clicks shut. Alone, except for the recording camera
in the upper left corner of the room, I almost lose control and
break down. I fight back the tears and slow my breathing.

There is no way I can continue to deal with all this weirdness.

In the last month, I have blown up a friend's wedding to stop her fiancé from murdering her. I was nearly strangled to death by my former favorite professor after I confirmed he was a serial killer. Most recently, a casino reneged on a hundred-thousand-dollar winning bet I placed because my dealer was killed by a crazed gunman seconds after I won. It did not help that every witness scattered to the wind once the bullets started flying.

Now I have lost the gun that currently is of immense interest to the police for some reason unknown to me.

These events cannot be written off as lousy luck. The question is, what do I do about it?

A small man in his mid-fifties closes the door. "Miss Snow, I am Detective Keaton."

"Hi."

Keaton examines the lid of his coffee cup as he asks. "Did Officer Lancaster fill you in on why we need to talk?"

I begin to mention the gun and remember I need to be as sparing as possible with the information. "No, sir."

Keaton's green plastic-seated chair screeches as he pulls it to him. He casually places a size eight loafered foot on it. "Miss Snow, how do you know Champ Janikowski?"

"We have never been properly introduced. But I can tell you he wears a large class ring on his right hand. If you need proof, I can show you the bruise it made under my chin." I point to my neck.

"It is not a class ring. It is a state championship ring from his junior year in high school."

Ten years seems like a long time to be wearing a symbolic glory years trophy from high school. But it does seem about right for a man like Champ.

Keaton leans in until I can see every vein in his bloodshot brown eyes. "And I believe you meant to say Champ *wore* a large class ring."

I do not know if Keaton is a stickler for semantics or attempting to explain that Champ no longer walks amongst the living. In either event, Keaton is studying me like I'm the last of an endangered species.

Not responding to his correction is the safest course of action I decide. Leaning back in my chair, I try my best to appear mildly bored.

"How do you know, Ace Gilbert?"

"We just met last night."

"I am curious, Miss Snow. Perhaps they do things differently up in Alabama. You are from Alabama. Correct?"

I know he knows darn well where I'm from. He probably has a complete profile of me by now. "Yes."

Keaton props a hand on his leg. "Is it a customary practice to loan your gun to folks you have just met?"

Detective Keaton waits for an answer from me. His neck reddens. "Are you going to answer me?"

I put on my best surprised look. "I am so sorry. I thought the question was rhetorical."

"I assure you nothing I ask you during this interview will be rhetorical." He stares at me then turns his hands over. "Well? Is that a general practice where you come from?"

"I would say typically no."

A slight smile flickers across his face. "So, it is not unheard of for people to loan guns out to people they have just met?"

"Oh, *that* would not happen. It would not be typical for us not to know somebody who lives in our town. It's a pretty small town. Also, everybody has a shotgun in the house at the bare minimum. You can understand it also wouldn't be typical for someone to *need* a gun loaned to them."

I think Detective Keaton is already on to me as he lets out an exaggerated sigh. "I'm trying to establish your mindset."

"Regarding what?"

"Why you would loan a pistol to a man you just met."

What the heck? I suddenly put two and two together and am surprised I did not understand earlier. "You think I loaned my gun to somebody?"

"Did you?"

I shake my head. "Absolutely not. Lord, the only reason I carry that stupid thing is because my daddy insists upon it. He would skin me alive if I loaned my gun to a stranger. Why would I do that?"

"Maybe you wanted somebody killed?"

Detective Keaton's question—which sounds more like an accusation—knocks the breath out of me. I open my mouth multiple times and fail to make a sound.

Think, April. Get ahead of this curve. What are the facts?

It is evident by detective Keaton's innuendo that Champ Janikowski has been murdered. More significant, he has been killed with my forty-five, which was taken from the glove compartment of Norman's car.

This is so not cool.

"Maybe somebody who wore a large state championship ring. Somebody who had recently backhanded you onto a table with that ring?" Keaton continues to badger me.

I raise a finger. "Excuse me. Would that be a felony assault? Champ slapping the stew out of me."

"Could be," Keaton says as he shrugs his shoulders noncommittedly. "It could also be motive."

If this was not so serious, it would be funny. Detective Keaton is so cocksure of his theory, I can sense he believes he has me dead center. But there are plenty of holes in his hypothesis. The most glaring is, I am innocent.

I teepee my fingers together and lean in toward him. "Let me see if I understand this correctly. You think because I got backhanded by some guy in a bar dispute, I loaned my pistol to a stranger I just met that night to have them kill the guy who slapped me. Is that your story?"

"That's no story. That's the truth," Keaton insists.

I realize that if Detective Keaton ever had an intelligent thought, it would die of loneliness. "For the sake of argument. Let us assume I believe removing someone from the face of the earth is equal payback for being slapped. Tell me. Why in the heck I would loan the only gun that can be traced back to me to someone to do the deed?"

Keaton takes his time solving my riddle before he suggests.

"Criminals make mistakes all the time."

"Hmmm, and so do detectives." I wave my hand in the air. "Let's forget about all that for a second. I need you to listen to me. Under no circumstances did I loan my handgun to anybody. It was in the glove compartment of my uncle's car. Somebody took it. It is as simple as that."

Keaton's eyes narrow. "And you don't find it at all odd the pistol you conveniently left in the glove compartment for someone to take killed a man who hit you a few hours earlier?"

Detective Keaton has no idea how unfortunately odd my life is. "I would say it is a run of coincidences. But again, I did not loan my gun to anyone."

"You simply left it conveniently available for someone to take with them. To do the dirty work."

A tremor racks my body as I fight to maintain control. "Listen, this Janikowski dude, I don't know him. He had some sort of disagreement with somebody I had just met. Champ began to tap dancing on my new acquaintance's head. I tried to intervene, and Champ backhanded me.

"If it were a big enough deal for me to consider having him killed, why wouldn't I have called the police and reported the incident?"

"To take care of it yourself later. Some people get off on being vigilantes."

I accidentally laugh. "You cannot be serious. First off, to be a vigilante, I would have had to kill him. Sending a friend to kill him would not have been a vigilante act.

"Second, it was a disagreement that turned momentarily violent. Then it was diffused. It really was no big deal."

"You say you did not loan anybody your gun. Then why did you put it in the glove compartment? Is that where you normally keep it? In the glove compartment of your uncle's car?"

"No."

"Then why was it there?" I don't answer, and he reiterates louder, "Why was your gun in the glove compartment, Miss Snow?"

I have been thinking about why I put the gun in the glove compartment since I realized it was missing. While I grew up with guns and carried my forty-five all through college because my daddy wanted me to have adequate protection, last night was the first time I drew it out of my purse.

It scares me to no end how close I came to dropping Champ Janikowski. No matter if he deserved it or not. I know deep down inside, I never could forgive myself if I had pulled the trigger and taken his life last night.

"I put it in the glove compartment because I did not want to carry a gun with me anymore. I concluded it could turn an unpleasant situation into a catastrophe in seconds. I don't want to be a part of that."

Keaton drops his foot from the chair and leans onto the table. "But it did turn into a catastrophe. Didn't it? A well-liked local business owner is dead because of your carelessness, Miss Snow."

I stare dumbfoundedly at Detective Keaton. I'm saved by a clicking noise from the door. A tall man with receding gray hair comes in and holds the door open. "Keaton, let me have a word with you, please."

Keaton looks from me to the tall detective, then back to me. "We will continue this in a moment."

As the door clicks shut, I'm alone with my thoughts. This cannot be happening again. I wonder if I should quit discussing things with Keaton and lawyer up. But why lawyer up? I haven't done anything wrong.

Actually, I have done something wrong. A responsible gun owner would never have left a firearm in easy access for someone. Especially someone who just got their butt kicked by a man for no good reason.

I may not have pulled the trigger on Champ. Still, I sure as heck seem to have made it easy for Ace to off the Three Sheets to the Wind owner.

None of this is my fault. At least I can tell myself that if it makes me feel better. The fact remains my gun apparently killed

Champ. Though I did not pull the trigger, I certainly facilitated his murder. It's not fair, and it's not right. Still, it is the truth, and the police appear ready to hold me responsible regardless of the circumstances.

The door clicks open again. The tall detective enters with an elderly gentleman wearing the most preposterous yellow bowtie I believe I have ever seen. "Miss Snow, your attorney has arrived."

Attorney? Is my appointed defense attorney, Mr. Magoo? With an improbably huge, yellow bowtie? That is odd. I did not even request an attorney yet.

The older gentleman lays a well-worn brown leather portfolio on the desk and makes a show of snapping the locks. "April, I am here on request of your uncle. I will help you navigate the situation."

"You are?"

He extends a hand, and I shake it. His palm is exceptionally soft and warm.

His cobalt-blue eyes are striking. "Yes, dear. My name is Benny Broadway. Your uncle and I go all the way back to law school together." He turns from me and asks the tall detective, "Cameron, are y'all planning on charging my client?"

Cameron runs a hand through his gray hair. "Benny, we were not exactly done interviewing her yet."

Benny smiles pleasantly. I have a feeling it is placating at best. "Your interview is complete, Cameron."

"We are considering charging her with negligence with a firearm."

Benny forms an "O" with his lips and shakes his shoulders. "Oh, my. The terrible 'negligence with a firearm.' Tell me, do you charge every homeowner with that when their gun is stolen?"

"Benny, this is different. Her gun was in a car."

"Right. And it being in a car is far more negligent than being in a house. Cameron, out of curiosity, the handguns you take in during the arrest of gang members and thieves. What percentage of them are stolen out of cars?"

Cameron shifts his weight. "Benny, I don't see what that has to do with your client."

"Oh, come now, Cameron. You are a smart man. What do you think I am alluding to?"

Cameron looks at me. "Miss Snow, can you promise me you will remain in town and be available over the next few weeks in case we have more questions?"

I start to answer, and Benny interjects, "Miss Snow does not reside in Florida and therefore cannot make that promise. In addition, short of a subpoena, we will not be answering any questions anyway."

Cameron appears ready to argue and then decides against it. "Very well then. Miss Snow, you can go now."

Cameron exits the room.

"Who sent you?" I ask Benny.

"I told you, your uncle." He stands and snaps his briefcase closed. Looking up, he understands my confused expression. "Oh, dear. Your uncle Howard called me after Norman called him and mentioned you needed legal representation."

"Oh."

"Let's not talk here, though. Have you had lunch yet, dear?"

"No, sir."

He gives me a brilliant smile, and his eyes draw me in like a magnet. "Excellent. I know a quaint little sushi bar just down the street. It will allow us to bring each other up to speed and enjoy a pleasant meal together, dear. Killing two birds with one stone, as they say." He favors me with a sly grin. "I suppose we should not speak of killing things given our present location."

On the way out of the police station, I see Norman talking with a gentleman in an office through a large plate of glass. Good, I do not consider myself high maintenance, but I had begun to feel slightly abandoned. I had not seen Norman before now, and he had promised to follow me to the station.

I catch his eye. Norman signals for us to wait. Seconds later, he comes down the hallway. "Is everything good, Benny?"

"I believe so. I am not positive what their angle is, but the case is crepe paper-thin."

Norman extends his hand to Benny, and they shake. "I appreciate you taking time to come over from Mobile."

"Think nothing of it. Besides, it allows me to go to my favorite sushi bar with the most beautiful company. April and I are going now. Would you like to accompany us?"

Norman puts on a gracious, if not honest, smile. He only eats fish if it is double battered and deep-fried. Sushi is not his thing. "As inviting as that sounds, I am about to get some information on the young gentleman who took April's gun and committed the crime."

"He didn't do it, Uncle Norman."

Norman studies me carefully in his detective manner, then frowns. "It's tough to accurately judge people's character, April. Especially people we have not spent much time with."

"No." I shake my head. "I'm positive Ace is not capable of killing someone."

"You would be amazed at what people can do when they feel threatened."

"That is true. *Very* surprising," Benny interjects.

"Besides, the timeline fits. Ace had the motive," Norman continues.

"But you know how easy it is for people to make assumptions," I plead. "Not having an alibi during the time of death and the victim having recently tap-danced on your head is not conclusive evidence. It is just circumstantial."

"Right, but then there is the security recording. Not to mention your friend resisted arrest and threw a punch at one of the arresting officers."

Everything changes at that moment. I feel my gut sink to the floor.

If the police have a recording of Ace near Champ's home at the time of death—being honest with myself—even my belief will be swayed. When we dropped Ace off, I assumed he was going to bed. He had no reason to be out that late unless he attempted to settle the score with Champ.

One last glimmer of hope flashes across my mind. "Did they

swab him for gunshot residue?"

Norman sucks in his lips and nods his head slightly. "I'm afraid so. He came back positive. Ace claims he and his roommate went to the armory this past weekend and did some target practice with some rentals."

Even if that is true, it is not helpful. In fact, I now wonder if Ace may have gone to the range to have a plausible reason for gunshot residue on his hands once he was arrested.

Maybe I am wrong about Ace. It is not like I know him. Perhaps this argument with Champ had been an ongoing situation, and Ace planned on killing Champ all along.

But my gun? There is no way he could know my weapon would be available.

Unless—my blood pressure shoots out the roof as I ask. "Did Ace say I gave him the gun? Is that why they called me down here?" By gosh, if that is the case. Ace better hope they put him behind bars for a long time, so I can't get to him.

"The exact opposite. Ace continues to insist you never knew he took your gun. Because of the witnesses who saw Champ strike you, the police think you might have asked Ace to kill Champ," Norman says.

"If he claims he did not kill Champ. Why did he take my gun?"

"He told the officers he was scared." Norman shrugs his shoulders. "Ace said he had never seen Champ that angry before and feared Champ might come to pay him a visit and finish what he started."

There are too many conflicting details in the story. I am getting the "can't see the forest for the trees" myopic vision.

Norman gives me a shoulder hug, something we are both a bit awkward with, and says, "Don't try to apply logic to crazy, April. It will drive you crazy."

I wonder if his sage advice is a little late for me.

"You go and enjoy your lunch with Benny. I will see you back at the condo tonight." He gives me a light pat on the shoulder as he turns back down the hallway.

"Shall we?" Benny says with a wave of his hand toward the

exit.

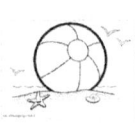

Chapter 9

Lunch fits perfectly with my standard theory of life. When troubled or in doubt, eat.

The Asian fusion restaurant Benny takes me to has only ten booths. I must admit, I have not been the biggest sushi eater in the world. Still, there is something about Benny that makes me want to spend a little time finding out more about him.

I order a California roll. Because it is the only sushi I have ever eaten. Initially, I picked it because I figured Californians might know a lot about sushi.

Benny orders four different rolls claiming I need to expand my sushi horizons. He also orders us a couple of sakes.

"Your uncle, Howard that is, tells me you plan on working for Master, Lloyd, and Johnson," Benny says as he liberally spreads spicy mustard on a spring roll.

"Yes, sir. I am one of two candidates selected for employment this summer."

Benny bites into his spring roll then sucks in air liberally as he chews. He has enough hot mustard for an entire spring roll on the one bite.

"I am planning on moving to Atlanta in two weeks. That will give me time to set up the week before I start to work."

"I assume you did due diligence before accepting the offer. Firms are rarely what they seem."

Here we go again. Howard has warned me about Master, Lloyd, and Johnson from the first time I mentioned their interest in me. "Yes, sir. They do a healthy business in Atlanta with high profile clients."

Benny favors me a smile, which appears more sympathetic than humorous. "Yes, dear. I am well aware of who they are. I was asking if *you* knew."

I pick up my spring roll and pour soy sauce on it, which promptly runs out the bottom. "So, were you a classmate with my uncle Howard?" I'm not the best at identifying people's age. Still, Benny looks a few years older than my uncle.

"I was a teacher's aide when Howard was a student at the University of Alabama. I am a good bit older since I served two tours in Vietnam before beginning college on the GI bill."

It may be rude, but I take an appraising look at Benny. "No offense, but wouldn't that make you in your seventies?"

He chuckles. "Seventy-two, to be exact. But who is counting?"

"I guess I am. If I was seventy-two, I would already be retired."

"That is easy to say when you are young. But I have a small practice in Mobile, which holds my interest. It is significantly less stressful than when I was a judge advocate."

"Seriously?"

"It is not as glamorous as it sounds, I assure you. Most jobs in life are not."

Now Benny is just being modest. Judge advocates in my book are the Blue Angels of the legal world. No, they do not make serious bank. But they get some incredibly complex cases at an unbelievably early age.

"Tell me about this young man you befriended who has stirred up the dust."

I rack my brain for the name of any guy I have dated as I wonder exactly what all Howard has told Benny about me. It reminds me of how pathetic my love life is. "What young man?"

"The young man who used your gun to murder the owner of Three Sheets to the Wind."

Oh, that guy—Ace. "I really only met him last night."

The waitress brings our sushi rolls. Benny thanks her and remains silent for so long after she leaves I believe he has dropped the subject of Ace.

"Did you loan him your gun?" he asks as he spreads a liberal amount of wasabi on his roll.

"No. I absolutely did not."

Benny pops the slice of sushi in his mouth. His eyes open wider. Benny obviously has a penchant for living on the culinary wild side.

As Benny gains control and drinks half a glass of water, he continues the conversation. "It is not a good situation. The Janikowski family is well known in Pensacola. Champ's dad owns several bars, and Champ inherited Three Sheets to the Wind a few months back. Your friend killed the owner of a trendy bar who was a member of a well-connected 'old' Pensacola family."

"And that somehow makes killing him worse?"

Benny favors me the same sympathetic smile he used earlier. "No, dear. It means the murder is high profile, and the police will be forced to find the murderer and bring them to justice. This is not a crime that lends itself to fading quietly with time."

Oh, and then there is that. I suppose Benny does make sense.

"Fortunately for you—even though he may be a murderer—your friend Ace is not a snitch. He did not implicate you in any way."

"He is not my friend. I just met him last night. And besides, he can't be a snitch if I did not do anything wrong."

"I would be less than honest if I claimed to believe leaving a gun in the glove compartment is responsible. But who am I to judge?"

The fact that Ace did not throw me under the bus when he could cut himself some slack makes me think about his character. I know I only met him by way of a few short hours. Still, the one thing I keep coming back to as a truth is Ace is incapable of killing anyone. At least in cold blood. Which is what I assume happened with my gun.

"What will happen to Ace?"

Benny takes his time and appears to contemplate the question entirely. "I say given the fact he was attacked by Champ, and there are multiple witnesses, that will play into the state's favor proving he killed Champ. However, it is a double-edged sword. It also proves Ace may have committed the crime under extenuating circumstances. Even though it was not in the heat of the moment, a jury may find him guilty of second-degree rather than first-degree murder. If that is the verdict. I believe your friend will serve twenty to thirty years and be eligible for parole after possibly half the sentence served for good behavior."

I do not believe I could have had a more visceral reaction if Benny told me the police would take Ace outside and shoot him in the head after his sentencing. Twenty to thirty years? I cannot even wrap my mind around the length of the sentence Benny predicts. It might as well be a death sentence.

"There is no way Ace did this."

Benny nods his head. "People can be unpredictable at best. And especially if embarrassed and humiliated in public. There is no telling what somebody might do."

"But I am telling you he is not that sort of person."

"Maybe not. But from what I understand, the police have some very compelling evidence."

"The recording?"

Benny exhales, and his expression becomes grimmer. "My understanding is the footage shows Ace entering Champ's apartment."

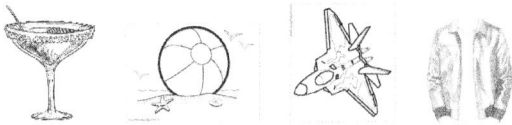

Benny gives me a ride back to the condo. I repeatedly run his statement about the security footage through my mind as we cruise in his red BMW.

It is incredible how advanced security monitoring and investigative techniques have become in the last ten years. It is nearly impossible for criminals to conceal their crimes now. With se-

curity cameras catching our every movement during the day—
not to mention the advancements in DNA testing—it is a wonder
any current crimes go unsolved.

This poses a predicament for me. I know at his core, Ace is primarily good. It is highly improbable anyone of his nature could
be a murderer. He certainly should not be capable of a homicide
that required him to steal a weapon, drive to his nemesis's home,
and kill him in cold blood.

Nope. Ace doesn't even have an eighth of the resolve and
meanness required for a semi-professional hit job.

But the surveillance footage shows him entering Champ's
home as advertised. That is what prosecuting attorneys like to
refer to as solid evidence. With the recording alone, even if Ace
was not found with the gun, my gun, on his person, a juror
would have to believe Ace killed Champ.

I know it is not my issue. But that does not stop the situation
from bothering me.

Benny pulls into our condo's driveway. "I don't want you talking with the police. If they call or show up at your door, I want
you to call me immediately. Do not say anything until I'm available."

"Yes, sir," I say with my hand on the car door.

"One last thing I feel I would be remiss if I did not mention."

I turn and give him my full attention. His hypnotic blue eyes
draw me in again.

"Working for a firm like Master, Lloyd, and Johnson may seem
exciting to you. Still, there are many positives to private practice
in a town where everybody knows and appreciates you."

Here we go again. My uncle must have requested his friend put
in another pitch for me working with him in Guntersville. As if
I am going to waste my life and talent in the small city I grew up
in.

"I know you believe you researched your new firm. Yet I have
heard some rumblings, and they are not good."

"I understand. But there are always people trying to knock
down the big firms. Isn't that just the nature of it?"

Benny favors me the same sympathetic smile, which conveys "oh, girl, you do not know the half of it" before he says, "Well, do not claim you were not warned."

"Thank you for lunch, the ride, and for the representation."

I leave Benny and his warnings as I step into the condo. I call out, but nobody answers. Don't they know I have been incarcerated and would really appreciate a coming home welcoming committee?

Is it too much for a girl to ask for? Apparently so. Fine, I don't have to be entertained twenty-four seven.

I grab my laptop and walk toward the back patio. My idea is to catch some sun while searching for a news article about Champ's murder.

Odd. There is no mention of Champ's early departure from the earth on social media. Even more disappointing, the surveillance recording the police case hinges on has not made it onto the web.

I should just give it all a rest, but it sure is peculiar. For Champ to be the supposed local hero, his death is not mentioned.

On a lark, I search Master, Lloyd, and Johnson. I did extensive research on the company when I applied for my position. My previous searches pertained to how the company treats its lawyers, client base, and information on their compensation package. For my interview, I also memorized the names of all the partners and junior partners of the firm.

My search brings up only one article regarding a complaint filed by a whistleblower concerning a recycling company that is a client of the firm. The whistleblower threw all manner of accusations at the recycling company, falling just short of accusing them of being in collusion with Doctor Doom. In addition to charging the recycling company, the prosecutor wants a piece of the owners and plant manager. For good measure, they're suing the company's law team, too.

There is nothing like making it personal with a behemoth law firm that practically controls the courts in Georgia. That lawsuit is not going anywhere.

It is so typical. When people decide to sue a company, they just go ahead and sue anybody who has anything to do with the company.

The sliding door to the apartment opens, and Trisha steps out. "Where is your phone?"

I did not realize it was not with me. "Inside, I guess."

She sits down next to me. "Guess who called?"

I hate the "guess who" game. "Blake Shelton."

"No, silly. I would not be here talking to you if that were the case," Trisha says without missing a beat. "Those pilot trainees that we met this morning."

I had totally forgotten about our yummy—if not a little too short—flyboy who chatted us up this morning. "What did they want?"

"It would seem they are dead set on taking us out. They asked if we would be interested in going to the waterpark tomorrow, and then catching an early dinner at Rippy's Tide."

I did like Wesley. But I need to figure out if there is any way I can help Ace. "Gee, I don't know, Trisha."

"Too bad. I already told them we would love to go."

"Well, thank you for checking in with my feelings on the matter first," I grouse.

"Oh, I know what your feelings are on the matter. I bet you have every inch of Mr. Wesley committed to memory."

"Please. Wesley is barely taller than I am."

Trisha rolls her eyes. "I swear, April May. You have got to be one of the finickiest girls in the world."

"You are so full of it." I am not finicky. I just have high standards. A man's height needs to be above a certain height, is all I'm saying. Besides, I did not come to Pensacola looking for a guy. I'm perfectly fine leaving Pensacola without one. "Besides, what happened with your Ace infatuation?"

"What gave you the idea I was attracted to Ace?"

"I don't know. Possibly the way you were fawning all over him."

"What?" Trisha attempts to look offended. She is a terrible actress. "I had no interest in Ace. I was not attracted to him in the least."

"Do not lie to me."

"I'm not. Geez, the only reason I was 'fawning' over him is that you almost killed him. I would not have given him the time of day if I did not believe you might end up being charged with assault."

"Your fears are unwarranted. Apparently, Three Sheets to the Wind is the last place in the world you will be charged with a felony assault." My tone is entirely too bitter.

Trisha grimaces. "I almost forgot. How did that go? Dad said Uncle Howard sent his friend to fix it for you."

Benny comes to mind with his over-the-top yellow bowtie, and I smile. "Yeah, his friend is a good lawyer. A nice man, too. He even took me to lunch. I like sushi. Who knew?"

Trisha sits on the lounge chair in front of me. "Two guys in one day? See, that is what I am talking about. You always have guys wanting to take you to lunch."

I consider explaining that Benny is three times my age but slap her thigh instead. "I cannot believe you did not ask me about my day at the police station *first!*"

Her nose wrinkles. "As if. Carry your stupid phone with you. I got distracted after I tried to call a few times. Besides, I knew Dad would take care of you."

"I'm afraid there is no fixing it for Ace. Norman says there is a recording of Ace skulking around Champ's home and maybe even breaking in."

"We already talked about it. My dad carries *his* phone." She raises her eyebrows.

The thought pops into my mind. Trisha will be an excellent helicopter mom someday.

"It is sort of exciting, though."

I'm not expecting that comment from her and laugh. "Exciting?"

"Sure. We hung out last night with a cold-blooded killer. Crazy, right? I mean, I feel like Bonnie and Ace is our Clyde."

"Ace is our nothing." I shake my head. "Honestly, Trisha. You ain't right."

"Come on. You have to admit it is exciting. Our lives are mostly all work, and this is a total rush!"

I've got excitement in spades. In fact, if I have any more drama in my life, my next apartment is liable to come fully furnished with pleasantly padded walls. "You really should take up rock climbing or sky diving if you need some excitement. Besides, I don't think Ace is the murdering type."

"And yet he did it."

There is that. "Yep."

"Dad said they might not have caught him, except someone vandalized Champ's house last week and spooked his wife. Champ just put the security camera system in." Trisha's expression lights up. "How unbelievable is it that Champ put in the security cameras just in time to catch his own murder."

"Technically, they did not film his murder, just his murderer. The only thing I find unbelievable about the whole thing is how incredibly unlucky Ace is."

"I know. But if he did the crime. He has gotta do the time."

True, but even with the evidence, I still have something in my gut telling me Ace isn't guilty. No, not a psychic vision. I would not mind getting one for once in my life if it could clear up my situation. Unfortunately, this is just a good old-fashioned hunch. "Hey, where were you while I was down at the police station?"

"Wouldn't you like to know?" Trisha says with a tone I'm sure she thinks is playful. I simply find it irritating.

I give her a droll stare until she cracks.

"So, I thought while you and Dad were down at the police station I would do some investigating on my own."

I swear it feels like someone just grabbed my heart and squeezed. "What do you mean investigating?"

"Think about it. We are on the front line of a first-degree murder case. The police are looking for the murderer of a popular local business owner. Who better to solve it than the people who were with the police's number one person of interest all last night?"

"The police."

Trisha waves her hand. "Please. I could have the whole thing solved by the time they complete a suspect list."

I narrow my eyes. "Did you hit your head or something?"

"No, silly. It is just heady stuff to think I may solve a murder mystery."

My cousin is a smart girl. There is no denying her intelligence. Especially if you consider she makes high grades in her law classes while working full-time and barely studying. Still, there are times when her judgment is decidedly irrational and overly spontaneous. She's like the girl who never drinks and then downs five shots of tequila one after another. The same smart girl, but her decision-making process is a little impaired.

Stress and excitement always have an odd effect on her cognitive abilities. She must have been overstimulated last night by the pressure of the fight and then the excitement from the police visit this morning.

"Trisha, I need you to calm down and tell me exactly what you mean by investigating?"

She flashes a coy grin. "I figure, usually in these types of murders, the best person to look at is the spouse." She lifts her hands and drops them by her side. "I mean, hello, did anybody talk to his wife?"

I close my eyes. "Please tell me you did not talk to Audrey Janikowski."

"Well, no."

"Thank the Lord for small favors."

"I was going to, but I staked out her house all day. She never showed up." She huffs. "So, of course, I was not able to talk to her. But doesn't that seem sort of sketchy that she never came home today?"

You would have thought it was Trisha who Champ backhanded last night. "No. I am quite sure if my husband were shot to death in our home last night, I would not bother coming to get my things. I'm surprised the police don't have the house still roped off."

"Oh, they do. One even came up to ask me what I was doing."

"Do you not understand how suspicious that looks? It is not unheard of for murderers to return to the scene of the crime."

She grins. "That is funny. That is exactly what the police officer said."

Trisha is making my head hurt. I feel like someone is on the inside of my brain, poking needles through the backside of my eyeballs. "Please tell me you left after that."

"Yeah. I got tired of waiting on her. So, I decided to drive by Ace's apartment?"

"Why?"

"I don't know. I just wanted to see if I got the 'killer impression' when I drove by his house."

Trisha, you beautiful, intelligent, and resourceful girl. Why didn't I think of that first?

It did not work for me in the Penny Trickett case, but she was not killed in her home. Professor Rosenstein killed her at his house and staged her suicide at her home.

We know Champ was killed in his house. If there had not been blood splatter from the forty-five, the police would not have kept saying he was killed in his home.

"Nobody was at his apartment. I went up to it and put my hand on the front door. That is when I felt it. Something dark and sinister, and now I know. Ace really did kill Champ."

To my knowledge, neither Trisha nor Norman has any psychic abilities. "Are you saying you are psychic now?"

She shakes her head and laughs. "Like that old show *The Medium*? No. I don't believe in paranormal stuff. I'm just saying the door felt evil somehow."

Which would be classic low-level psychic capabilities. *If* Trisha really sensed negative energy, and it was not a contrived feeling she built up over the sorrow of somebody she liked being charged with murder. In either case, even though it is vital to investigate further, I need to table the discussion for now.

"Trisha, did the police officer tell you how long they plan to have the home locked down?"

She frowns. "No, but I didn't ask. Why?"

"How many police were out there?"

"The police officer, and I think two CSI personnel. Why?"

The sliding glass door opens. Norman pokes his head through the opening. "I'm sick of fried fish. What do you say we get a couple of pizzas?"

I jump to my feet, closing my laptop with a snap. "That sounds awesome. I'm starved."

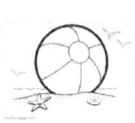

Chapter 10

Tony's Pizzeria and Pasta has been a favorite of the Snow-Hirsch clan for as long as I can remember. What it lacks in taste, it makes up for in sentimental value.

The pizza is marginally better than frozen pizzas from the supermarket. The marinara sauce tastes suspiciously like ketchup. Still, it is one of the first non-seafood-oriented restaurants on the Gulf Breeze side of the bridge. Tony's is always reliable when we need to break up the monotony of seafood restaurants.

Besides, it offers all-you-can-eat complimentary garlic cheese toast. Who doesn't like garlic cheese toast?

I'm halfway through my Caesar salad—more Caesar dressing than salad—when Norman speaks up, " I have a big surprise for you girls."

I'm twenty-seven years old. Still, I get butterflies in my stomach, and I feel my face stretch into a wide goofy grin. Seriously, what surprise can Norman give me to justify my giddiness?

Trisha leans across the table. "You got us tickets to this weekend's battle of the bands?" Trisha guesses.

"Better. One of the guys who went through police training with me in Nashville transferred down here ten years ago." Norman points to me. "That is who you saw me talking to at the police station, Trisha."

I give a quick nod of my head while I continue to grin like a fool.

"One of his daughters lives in Orlando, and she is nine months pregnant. If she does not go into labor by this weekend, they are going to induce labor."

My smile begins to falter. Trisha and I share a look, and she shrugs.

"With that going on, he will not be able to use his tickets this weekend." Norman stops, smiles, and takes a swig of beer.

"Tickets for what, Dad?" Trisha asks the obvious.

"The Pink Pufferfish," Norman says emphatically.

Trisha's eyebrows knit together. "Is that like an eighties hair-band or something?"

I exhale loudly and release the last of my strained smile. "They are a Minor League baseball team."

Trisha tries to recover and smile. It does not reach her eyes. "Awesome, Dad."

I am not exactly the "keep a scorecard" type of girl myself. Still, there are many worse things in life than sitting outside watching a bunch of athletic men in their prime running around in tight white pants while I enjoy a foot-long cheese dog. It is a secret vice of mine I developed while pitching in little league baseball. Who knew watching boys and letting my imagination run wild is often much more enjoyable than actually dating them?

"Absolutely unbelievable seats. His tickets are four rows up be-hind third base."

I try not to laugh. That is an excellent place to get beaned by a foul ball. Trisha will love this.

"That is great, Dad. It is awfully nice of him to offer."

"Yep. We even have a parking pass. You girls be ready to go at five o'clock on Friday."

"We'll be ready," I say.

Our waitress removes our salad plates and brings more fresh bread. I'm on my second slice when Norman clears his throat.

"April, about your gun. The police are going to be keeping it for evidence," he says.

"I figured as much. I don't really want it back anyway."

"I understand. I'm not sure I would want it back, either." He sighs. "I know he was only an acquaintance, but I truly am sorry about your friend. It is an unpleasant situation. Plenty of witnesses confirm the story that Champ attacked Ace at the bar. The two of you were only attempting to defend yourself. And then you left as quickly as possible."

"Did you talk to Ace?" I ask.

"No. It would not have been appropriate."

I stare at my warm garlic toast and tear it apart. "Ace did not do it. I am sure of it."

"April, how many times do we have to go over this? They have him on film," Trisha interjects.

I ignore her. "You saw the recording. Right, Norman?"

Our waitress brings our order. Norman squints his eyes, signaling for me to be quiet for a moment. As she hands out our plates, I wonder why I'm even having this conversation. Ace is not my responsibility. The police will do a thorough job, and the truth will come out. They will only bring charges against Ace if they have rock-solid evidence.

As the waitress leaves our table, Norman leans forward. "Yes. Stephen, that's my buddy who used to work in Nashville, allowed me to see the surveillance recording."

"But you did not talk to Ace?"

"No, honey. There is no reason the police would let me talk to Ace."

"So, how do you know it was him? In the surveillance recording."

Norman starts to answer me and pauses. "Stephen told me it was him."

I smile as we lock eyes.

"Never take someone else's word for something you can prove yourself," Norman says slowly.

"Your words, not mine," I say. "I need to see that recording."

Norman stabs at his calzone. "I never thought when I taught

you girls the basics, you would turn my words on me."

"You should be honored we remembered those lessons all these years," I say.

"Sure, this is me looking honored." Norman gives a disingenuous smile before taking a massive bite of his calzone and chewing in exaggerated motions.

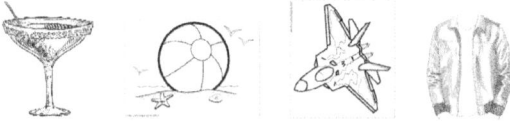

I cannot fall asleep. I stare at the reflection of the digital clock on the ceiling, watching it turn minute by minute. I have a difficult decision to make, and it is eating me from the inside out.

My family believes doing the right thing always takes precedence over the most expedient or convenient course of action. Believe me, it aggravates me to no end some days to be from a family of do-gooders. If it were not for my upbringing, I'm unsure who I would be.

But it's hard to shake off a lifetime of social training.

It is not even a fair comparison, though. Me doing what I know is right is not just an inconvenience. It could cost me my sanity.

No, really. I think back to the recent incident in the old town cemetery in Biloxi, Mississippi. I followed a ghost, like a fool, into a graveyard in hopes I would better understand her plight and help her.

No good deed goes unpunished, as my Nana likes to joke.

Everything was fine as I entered the cemetery and located the burial location of the ghost I followed. When I attempted to leave the grave, the entire world tilted, and I feared for my life.

Literally, the graveyard gate spun in the opposite direction as I tried to escape. Then an ancient oak in the center began to move as if it were formed by a column of human bodies all struggling to reach out and touch me as I passed by. When the first graves collapsed inward and others became quicksand traps, my panic hit full throttle. I believe I even quit breathing.

I'm still unsure how I escaped. I have no idea what would have become of me if I had not. But I'm sure if something did not kill me first, my sanity would have snapped like an overstretched rubber band if I had stayed in the graveyard for a few more minutes.

Starting with my friend Susan's wedding a month ago, my psychic abilities have spiked upwards in both intensity and regularity.

Then there are the first three days of my vacation in Pensacola —nothing. No random voices from dead people, and believe me, Pensacola is an old enough city for that to be a valid concern. It would be more probable than not for me to pick up a stray voice now and again. I had not even received any accidental readings from being close to or inadvertently touching someone.

I even began to believe two weeks in Pensacola would allow my psychic, mental muscle to atrophy. Then when I move to Atlanta, as long as I remain cognizant of not bringing it back to life or waking it, I might be rid of my "gifts."

Then Ace grabbed my hand, and everything flooded back. I think it may be one of the reasons why I had such an adverse reaction to Ace. It really upsets me to no end after three restful days of solitude from my "gifts," Ace managed to mess it up. In a matter of seconds, he crashed my hopes of being rid of my psychic abilities.

Now, once again, Ace is threatening my opportunity to be normal. I'm really starting to despise him.

I roll over onto my side and punch my pillow hard and then again harder. Stupid Ace. What in the world did he do to get Champ so fired up? He claimed Ace said something to his wife. I don't even know when he would have spoken to Audrey.

Ace was with me before Champ came in with his redheaded bride. It must have been a tragic case of mistaken identity.

Gosh, I don't want to do this. But between my family training of helping people when I can, plus my own curiosity, I'm afraid I will make one of the worst decisions of my life. It's been on my mind ever since Trisha said she put her hand on Ace's door. I need to get into Champ's house and investigate any residual energy imprints. If there are any, they might supply me with a clue.

Even if the energy fields tell me the police have the right culprit in Ace, at least I can be sure. I am still having a challenging time believing that Ace killed Champ. Not because of some evidence I have, just my feeling of who Ace is, and what he is and is not capable of. He can be a complete pain in the backside, but I just do not think he's a killer.

I'm also looking forward to reviewing the security recording tomorrow. Norman promises he will go to the station and try to secure a copy of the video from Stephen on a thumb drive. Hopefully, Stephen will be understanding.

I roll onto my stomach and try to distract myself with thoughts about our double date tomorrow with the flyboys from the base. It has been a long time since I have been on a date. It is exciting, even though I realize it's just a temporary fling. There is nothing wrong with spending a day with a guy who thinks enough to call you after you more or less summarily dismiss him because of an emergency.

My chest tightens as butterflies tingle in my stomach. I guess Lieutenant Junior Grade Wesley really does like him some April. That is pretty cool.

Chapter 11

"Trisha, hurry it up. They are here," I holler up the stairs. For the life of me, I do not know why she thinks she needs to put on the full complement of makeup. We are going to a waterpark, not a bar.

I open the front door. "Hey, guys, come on in. We're almost ready." Goodness, Wesley is so attractive it almost hurts to look at him. It's like he is a fusion of a rugged MMA fighter and metro refinement. How can that even be possible?

"We sure are glad this worked into your schedule," Hank says.

"Bah, we're on vacation. We don't have a schedule. You guys are the ones with the real job and training to work around." I notice Wesley staring at me intently. I wish I had used more concealer for the bump on my chin. "Earth to Wesley."

He shakes his head and smiles. "I apologize. You are so beautiful I didn't realize I was staring. I could look at you all day."

For once in my life, I'm speechless. I have had men compliment me in a similar manner as part of a pickup line often enough. Those I can easily swat back to the guy with a snarky jab. Wesley is only speaking his truth. It discombobulates my brain and sends every cell in my body humming. "Thanks," I manage to croak.

Thankfully, Trisha comes jogging down the stairs two at a time. "Sorry, I'm late."

Hank stands firm, his mouth parts as his eye widen. Trisha places her hand on his chest as she cocks her head. "Are you alright, Hank?"

Hank's ears flush red. "Wow," he whispers.

Trisha turns to me with a quizzical expression on her face. As usual, she is clueless that her date is awestruck by her. "Hail, hail, the gang's all here," I say as I pick up my keys. The tinkling sound of my keys brings Hank back to the present.

Trisha and I lock up and follow the guys to their Jeep. Wesley gets in to drive. I take shotgun while Trisha and Hank get in the back.

It has been a long time since I rode in a Jeep. I already like this date.

"I hope you don't mind that we took the side panels off. We thought it would be a wonderful day for it if the rush of wind messing up your hair does not bother you," Wesley says.

"I live for the feel of the wind blowing through my hair." Don't ask. I have no idea where that came from. Feeling awkward, I add the more common, "Beach hair, don't care."

Wesley turns in his seat and grins. "You are truly a woman after my heart, April."

My plan was never to be after Wesley's heart. Still, something odd is happening inside me. Maybe I am after his body.

I pull my emotions under control during our thirty-minute ride to the waterpark. The extra-deep tread on the Jeep tires and the rush of wind at sixty miles an hour make any conversation impossible.

The noise drops considerably as we slowly enter the waterpark's lot. Trisha immediately begins talking ninety to nothing about random topics. She is in high-stress mode.

"I want to do the tower slide," she announces excitedly.

"Hmm—I will watch you go down it. But I'm not into wedgies," Hank says.

We walk toward the gate. Wesley takes my hand in his. I start to pull away, afraid I may read something from him since we have only recently met.

Instead of getting visions and snippets of thoughts, I experience a warm surge of energy that flows through my body, forcing me to smile. I steal a look at Wesley, and he returns a smile. Without thought, I tighten my grip on his hand. I do not believe holding hands has ever felt so natural to me.

Trisha does brave the tower slide. As Hank predicted, she ended up with a wedgie and a bikini top malfunction.

As for me, I have a complete blast following Wesley's lead to every inner tube and foam mat ride in the waterpark. We race each other on the single mats and strain to get every ounce of speed out of the double inner tube ride. I can't remember the last time I laughed this much.

As I sit reclining on my inner tube in the lazy river holding his hand, Wesley rubs his foot up and down the back of my calf. Typically, this much intimate body contact causes my stress level to spike. Whenever Wesley touches me, I only feel the same positive energy flow. I just want more of it.

"I have enjoyed being with you today."

His statement catches me off guard. "I bet you say that to all the girls."

He rolls his eyes. "I'm afraid you have got the wrong guy, Miss Snow. I will admit I usually find the fairer sex, shall we say, more trouble than what they are worth."

"That is a sexist thing to say, Mr. Greenwood," I tease.

"You are different, April. I can't put my finger on it, but I felt comfortable with you the first time I talked to you."

The cells in my body begin to hum again. As pleasurable as it feels, I'm suddenly concerned. "Me too. It is a shame we both have goals that will take us to cities thousands of miles away from each other."

Wesley removes his foot from my leg. I miss his touch immediately. "And that is why we live for today," he says.

I would like to, but I am afraid of what heartache tomorrow will bring.

After the waterpark, the boys take us to a beachside barbecue and fish fry dive called Rippy's Tide. Obviously, a play on the word riptide and the fact the owner has more University of Alabama Crimson Tide memorabilia than most frat houses in Tuscaloosa. I feel right at home.

"You think you are slick bringing me here. Don't you, mister?"

"How so?" Wesley smirks.

I wave my hand, pointing at the walls. "All the Alabama gear."

"I do my research. The guys at the base told me this place is great. I only hope all the Alabama pictures don't make me lose my appetite. I'm a Buckeyes fan myself."

"Oh, well. There is no point in us having dinner together. It would never work out." I feign as if to leave.

Wesley catches my hand. "You're brave enough to break bread with the enemy."

I yield to the warmth of his hand and give an exaggerated sigh. "I suppose I can make an exception this time."

"Besides, I have heard opposites attract. I'm not afraid of a challenge."

Wesley edges his head closer to me as he favors me with a sly smile. I feel a fissure in the wall I have built around my heart. Actually, I believe a whole side of the wall just collapsed.

Bless it. I pray Wesley is not really serious about me. At this moment, I do not trust myself to stay focused on my goals. The last thing I need in my life is a guy I am crazy about dragging me all over the country. That would make it particularly impossible to earn a partnership at a law firm.

Calm down, April. It's only a date.

Ordinary people have dates all the time. I don't need to do a strategic analysis of our long-term relationship viability as a couple. This relationship only needs to be workable for a few more hours for the date to be a complete success. Then I can tuck it away in my memory as one of the best days I have experienced in years.

Wesley orders some fried crab claws as an appetizer while we look over the rest of the menu.

"Trisha, what are you ordering?" Hank asks.

"I think I'm leaning toward the ribs."

She clearly has not thought her decision through. I'm planning on going with the grilled tuna sandwich, and I am already concerned whether I should pick it up or try to eat it with a fork and knife.

What is wrong with me?

"That sounds awesome." Hank taps the menu with his finger. "Look, we can get the sampler for two. Two racks of ribs, two half chickens, and two pounds of pulled pork."

"How big are those two people?" I ask.

"I'm game if you are," Trisha tells Hank.

Wesley lays his hand on mine, drawing my attention away from the couple. "Would you like a margarita or beer?"

"I'd better not for now."

Wesley raises his eyebrow. "Okay. But if you change your mind, don't hesitate."

April May Snow is one of the most socially adept people in the world. Yet suddenly, I am the awkward, too-tall sixth grader at my first middle school dance. I have no clue why I feel so out of sorts.

Well, I do know why. It's because of the ultra-attractive, easy to talk to young man sitting next to me, whom my body keeps moving closer toward without any conscious decision on my part.

But for the first time in ages, I feel self-conscious around a man. I know that is not normal for me, which indicates I may not be fully in control of my emotions ... and *that* petrifies me.

"Are you all right?" Wesley asks.

"Oh yeah." I flash a smile I hope does not appear as forced as it feels. "I'm just a little torn between a sandwich or a plate."

"I know what you mean. I can't decide between the tried-and-true blackened mahi mahi sandwich or this Cajun grouper pasta."

I'm mesmerized by how he studies the menu as his finger traces across the protective vinyl. He turns his golden hazel eyes to me, crashing into my bout of staring. I do a little jump in my seat as I feel a tingle below my navel.

Wesley pauses and his lips form a slight smile. "Should I go 'Mr. Conservative,' or 'wild and crazy'?"

"Definitely wild and crazy." My voice sounds breathy and sultry to me.

"I agree. Wild and crazy is always best." His expression makes him appear hungry. For me. "Otherwise, you might miss out on something delightful."

The intensity of his stare stokes a fire in my belly. I adjust in my seat as I look away.

April, what are you doing? Think of your career.

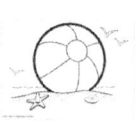

I learn a lot about Lieutenant JG Wesley Greenwood over the next two hours. I now know he grew up with four older sisters, and his dad was a Navy enlisted man who later worked the docks in Cleveland, Ohio.

Wesley was a baseball player in high school—I knew it—and he, like me, is a fan of the Blue Angels. If it were not for the fact that he is too short and I have got a lot of work to do to become the most sought-after defense attorney in the Southeast, we would be perfect for each other.

"I do not understand why you want to fly helicopters instead of jets if you are a Blue Angels fan."

Wesley leans back in his chair. "*Black Hawk Down.*"

"The movie?"

"I know it sounds stupid." He looks down at his hands.

"Not stupid. I'm just surprised."

"I just saw those ultra-cool helicopters in the movie. Right away, I thought to myself, I have got to fly one of those. So here I am."

"Are they hard to fly?"

He laughs. "I don't know. I'll tell you once we get there. That is enough about me. Tell me how April decided to become a lawyer."

"My uncle. Not Trisha's dad, my father's brother." Wesley's face pinches as if he is trying to figure out my family tree. "I know it's sort of a big extended family. There are a lot of folks to keep up with."

"You say that like it's a bad thing. It sounds pretty cool to me."

I swirl the last of the frozen margarita in my long-stemmed glass. I changed my mind shortly after dinner. "I think it's sort of like a double-edged sword. When you really need family, they are always there for you. Believe me, there are plenty of them. That also means when you need some time alone to figure something out, there are all these people trying to get into your business."

"I can understand that. You also seem like the type of woman who does not need people to be inserting themselves into her life of their own volition."

Turning, I give Wesley my best stink eye. "What is that supposed to mean?"

"Don't act like you don't know. I thought you were going to castrate me when I started talking to you on the beach."

"What?"

"Hank and I have battled seasoned trainers who come across as more accommodating than you."

"I'm not sure how I feel about you saying that."

He laughs. "Maybe not. But you know how I feel. I'm here because I thought you seemed worth risking castration."

"The night is young, and I still have my knife in my purse."

"I will remember that. What is your 'not Trisha's dad' uncle's name?"

"Howard. He is a defense attorney. Growing up, I appreciated that he helped people when they were accused of crimes. I have seen Howard help hundreds of folks out of bad situations. In several cases, people were charged with crimes they did not commit. They would have gone away for a long time. Except Howard was able to put a case together to get them exonerated."

Wesley nods his head. "That is pretty cool. I mean being able to help someone when they can't help themselves. I'm sure it would be terrifying if the whole judicial system came down on you, and you were innocent."

Just like that, Wesley gets it. He is not just saying it. Wesley understands. He seems to believe what motivates me to be a lawyer has value and makes sense. Why does his opinion matter to me so much? *I should not have drunk that second margarita.*

"And Howard is in Atlanta?"

"No. His practice is in Guntersville. My hometown."

"So, your grandmothers, brothers, parents, and your lawyer uncle who you talk so fondly about live in Guntersville?" Wes points in one direction with his right hand. He crosses it, pointing in the opposite direction with his left. "But you are moving to Atlanta."

When he puts it that way, it does sound odd. "It's complicated."

"It must be." He looks toward the band and dance floor. "Do you know what is not complicated?"

"No, but I hope you are about to tell me."

"The two-step."

I look out over the small dance floor where Trisha and Hank are dancing. They are a cuter version of Mutt and Jeff since Hank is well over a foot taller than Trisha.

"Yeah. I'm not really a two-step girl."

Wesley stands and holds his hand out to me. "Wow, a boy from Ohio who knows country dancing and a girl from Alabama who does not."

"I know country dances, buddy. I just said I don't two-step." Because I do not trust my treacherous body to behave if I get that close to Wesley right now.

"There is no such thing as a no-two-step girl. There are girls who two-step and girls who just have not found the right partner yet."

I have on wrinkled shorts, a damp T-shirt, no makeup, and my hair is going in five hundred different directions.

Worse, every inch of my body is moving like hot lava under my skin from pent-up sexual urges. Still, for some inexplicable reason, I take Wesley's hand and let him lead me out onto the dance floor. What sort of fool am I?

"I'm surprised you are not ashamed to be dancing with me," I say.

"Why in the world would you say that?"

I take my hand off his back and pat my hair. "Because you are dancing with the wild-haired lady."

"What happened to 'beach hair, don't care'?" he says with a laugh.

"I guess that was before I knew you were going to pull me in front of a crowd."

Wesley makes a show of scanning the room as we dance across the floor. "I don't see anybody here I know other than the folks who were in my Jeep. So, the crowd can keep their opinions to themselves."

I settle into the dance rhythm I know well and enjoy the simple pleasure of feeling my hand in his and his other hand on my waist. Dancing as a couple is as intimate as I feared. With our faces only inches away, I begin to commit his features to memory. I know fifty years from now, I will be able to recall every detail of Wesley as if I were still at Rippy's Tide, twenty-seven, and dancing in his embrace. I will see his sandy blond hair and how it sticks up from a cowlick in the most endearing way, his strong jawline darkened by the day's whisker growth, and most of all, his autumn gold hazel eyes. Yes. I would love to wake up to his beautiful face for a few decades.

"You are dead set on moving to Atlanta?"

I welcome the question that brings me out of my warm, fuzzy daydream. My mind was straying into dangerous territory as I was deciding if the sheets in our home would be ivory or powder blue. "Everything is done but the packing."

He looks away and says, "I don't suppose there is any way a guy could ever entice a power attorney like you to follow him around the world."

"Possibly."

"Really?" We stop dancing. "Tell me how."

"Well, if you are a world-renowned cupcake baker who owns a high-end ladies' shoe store, I can be persuaded."

Wesley tilts his head back and laughs. "So, that's the secret to it?"

"Yeah. I don't know why you guys act like women are such a mystery. A new pair of cute shoes and a fancy cupcake is all it takes."

Wesley starts us back around the floor. "That is valuable information. I appreciate you sharing it with me."

"I'm glad I could clear things up for you."

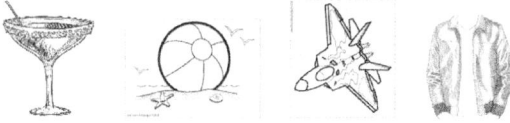

Chapter 12

The drive home is beyond awkward. The sexual tension between Wesley and me is the main reason.

Trisha and Hank, having thrown away all pretense of propriety, are making the situation even more uncomfortable. Their kisses are so loud from the back seat. I feel like they are echoing in my head. Even the hum of the Jeep's tires can't conceal the couple's wet, smacking noises.

"What do you think?"

Wesley's voice stirs me out of my irritation. "Regarding?" I ask.

"I'm trying to find out if we did well enough to score another date."

"Hmm, let me see. I was not keeping tally as we went along."

"Best date ever!" Trisha hollers in my ear. I'm surprised she could hear us talking, given her and Hank's antics.

"I guess you two survive and advance to the next round, then," I quip.

Wesley's right thumb taps the steering wheel in quick succession. "We will not be able to get off base until six tomorrow. Would that make it too late for a dinner date?"

I play it cool, lean back in my seat, and prop my bare feet on the dash. "You worry a whole lot. Don't you, Lieutenant?"

He looks surprised. With complete conviction, he says, "Only when the stakes are high."

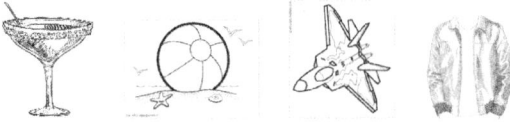

Trisha's words are slurred because she is brushing her teeth while she talks. "I can't believe you did not even kiss him. Is there something wrong with him?"

No. It's me. "I'm just a lot more cautious in relationships than you are."

Trisha's arm stops moving like a piston. She peers around the door casing. Her eyes narrow. "Excuse me?"

I'm not going to get away with that one. I have always been "the devil may care" of the two of us regarding men. Trisha usually, tonight being the exception, has always been a lot slower to initiate physical contact with men.

Trisha tucks her head back into the bathroom and spits out her toothpaste. She reappears, pointing her toothbrush at me. "You like him."

I look down at my phone. "He's okay."

"You never could lie."

I look her in the eye and focus hard. "Nobody is lying here."

She continues to stare. My sober expression transforms into a smile.

"Good thing you're not a spy. You would not live long." She returns to the bathroom and turns the faucet on.

"I can't help it if I have naturally high morals," I grumble.

Trisha turns out the bathroom light and gets into her bed. "Alright, Mother Teresa. Your loss." She pulls the covers up to her neck. "But I, for one, had an enjoyable time and am looking forward to some R-rated dreams."

Trisha is so blasted goofy. I love her for that. "Sleep tight."

"Don't stay up too late," she says with a breathy tone.

I can't tell Trisha, but I didn't kiss Wesley because I am afraid I would like it too much. I'm already out of control around him.

It's like I can't be close enough to him.

Given what our lives will look like shortly, Wesley Greenwood is an addiction I cannot afford. The best way to avoid getting hooked on something is to never try it.

Still, I doubt if my "just say no" idea will work. Lord knows I may be saying no, but my body's screaming yes, yes, YES!

Tomorrow night if I were to kiss him and I absolutely love it, what is the worst that could happen? Okay, but April Greenwood does not exactly sound awful. Right?

This is not like me at all. Guys do not have this effect on me; I have this effect on guys. I am not particularly fond of this whole "tables are turned" situation.

If I were smart, I would be sick tomorrow and not go out on the date. I'm definitely flying too close to the flame.

Ace pops into my head. Just a normal thought, nothing paranormal.

I'm ashamed. Here I am, sitting cross-legged on my comfortable bed, worrying if I'll kiss Wesley or not like some middle schooler. Poor Ace is lying on a wafer-thin mattress while the chain-link box springs cut into his skin, wondering if he will ever be released from prison.

I believe, unequivocally, he's innocent. Unfortunately for him, I'm not talented enough, not smart enough, or am too distracted to help him. I try to dismiss his predicament as not my issue because we barely know each other. But I may be his only hope. That means whether I can help or not, I must do what I can. I set my phone alarm and turn out the light.

Granny is who always preaches it's not whether you fail or succeed. It's whether you succeed in doing the best to your abilities. Sometimes being a responsible adult bites.

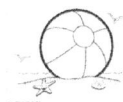

Chapter 13

I must be in heaven. The glorious smell of sausage fills the air. I open my eyes to find it still dark in our room. Being a hardcore carnivore, I get out of bed and pad into the kitchen despite still being sleepy.

Standing in the doorway, I watch my uncle for a few seconds then ask the obvious, "Why are you up so early?"

His back straightens as he turns quickly to face me. "You might as well be a ghost, April. I did not hear you get up."

"Is that biscuit gravy." I rub my eyes.

"Yes. I didn't mean to wake you girls. I was going to set your plates in the fridge so you could warm them in the microwave when you got up."

I shuffle to the bar stools and sit down. "It's never as good warmed up."

"True, but it is better than going hungry."

While I watch him work the stove and oven, my head bobs a few times. I wonder if I will fall asleep again. "So, why are you up early?"

"Stephen invited me on a deep-sea fishing charter with some of the other officers who are off today." He shakes his finger in the air. "That reminds me. I have something for you. Watch the eggs for me."

I groan on the inside as I push off the barstool and walk to the stove. It's not so much I don't want to help, even though I am incredibly groggy. It's just I have been known to burn bread regularly in a toaster. Not a toaster oven, a toaster. I don't want to screw up six scrambled eggs.

"Where is your laptop?" Norman asks. "You need it for this."

I start to ask what "this" is but decide that it would be rude if it is something I actually want. I move the eggs off the burner and go back to our room.

It is so dark in the room I can barely see. I stub my toe walking by Trisha's bed. Falling forward, I catch my balance by placing my hands roughly on her mattress.

"Is that sausage I smell, or did you leave your straightening iron on?"

"Your dad cooked breakfast. He is about to leave to go deep-sea fishing."

Trisha makes a slight grunting noise before slapping the covers off her. "Ugh, I better go tell him goodbye."

Picking up my laptop, I lament how much better a daughter Trisha is than me. It just comes naturally to her, I guess.

Norman takes the biscuits out of the oven as I return to the kitchen. He sets them down and pulls a thumb drive out of his shirt pocket. Holding it up to me at eye level, he says, "I never saw it, you never saw it, and it never existed."

He does not need to explain what he is holding. I know he has been able to come through with his promise of a copy of the surveillance recording from Champ's house the night he was murdered.

I pop the drive into the USB port and nearly curse with impatience as it takes forever to load.

Trisha sidles up to me with two mugs of coffee, sliding one next to my right hand.

The recording begins to play. I scan to the bottom right and see the entire clip is only a minute and five seconds.

The first half of the recording shows the motion sensor light turning on. The footage captures the image of Ace in a ball cap pulled low, walking the sidewalk in front of the house leading into the driveway. The second half shows him standing on the front porch and trying the doorknob.

Then it ends.

I play it again, and this time peculiarities hop out at me. First, Ace is wearing his aviator glasses, flight jacket, and Blue Angels ball cap. The exact same outfit he was wearing when we first met.

I recall wondering how Ace could move around the dimly lit bar with his sunglasses on. It would be impossible for him to see on the street at night with those dark sunglasses.

Sunglasses would make sense if he were trying to conceal his facial features. All I see is his chin and lips, void of any substantially distinguishing characteristics. If I were giving a police sketch artist a description, I would call his features "average." Not particularly helpful.

"It certainly looks like him," Trisha says.

"Or somebody trying to look like him."

Norman sets a plate in front of each of us. "Careful now. Don't let your conspiracy theories get the best of you."

"Something is not right, though," I say as I play the home security recording again.

Trisha loses interest and takes a seat. "Well, maybe you are right. But it sure looks like him to me."

"Even if it is him. This does not prove he is who killed Champ."

"No. But Ace does have a motive from the brawl at the bar. Once you marry that with proven opportunity, most juries will find him guilty."

Norman is right. The entire case hinges on this recording. Bless it. I thought getting a copy and seeing for myself would clear everything up. I thought if I saw Ace slinking around Champ's house, it would confirm that Ace is precisely where he needs to be—behind bars.

Instead, I am looking at a high-resolution, in-focus picture—Champ obviously took Audrey's concern to heart, not skimping on equipment—of someone who resembles Ace. Still, I cannot be sure.

"You said it is not as good warmed up." Norman gestures toward my plate. "So, get busy eating, young lady."

I hesitate before closing my laptop. Maybe if I take a break from it and come back later, I will see what fuels my doubts.

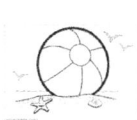

Unfortunately, the beach does not hold the same magical qualities today. It is the same pristine white sand, aqua-blue water with two-foot waves, and intriguing people strolling the beach. But I am a mass of aggravated electrons. I can't stop my hands and feet from bouncing. I feel as if I would run away at the first loud noise.

Trisha has been asleep under the umbrella for the last hour. I have been waiting patiently—well as patiently as I ever am—for her to wake up. I reach over and run my finger up her arm, touching only her ultra-fine hairs.

She slaps her arm. Scratching, she opens her eyes.

"Oh, good. You are up," I say.

Trisha scans side to side. "Is something the matter?"

"I was just thinking about Ace."

Trisha groans. "Give it up, April. You saw the recording."

"Yes, but I was thinking. Why didn't the footage show the killer entering Champ's house?"

Trisha squints her eyes. "I don't know."

"I mean, it *is* motion activated."

"Maybe the police cut that part out while they were editing it."

"Why would they do that? That would be better evidence than the rest of the video."

Trisha sits up and stretches her arms over her head. "I don't know, April."

"Don't you find it a little odd?"

"I guess."

"I need to go to Champ's house. I have a feeling if I go there, I will find the answer to why I do not feel right about the recording." I wait for her to say something. Instead, I get a droll stare. "Will you go with me?"

"Do I have a choice?" she asks sarcastically.

"I can go by myself. You did."

"I was not planning on going inside."

"Who said I was going inside?"

"You didn't have to. I know you," Trisha says.

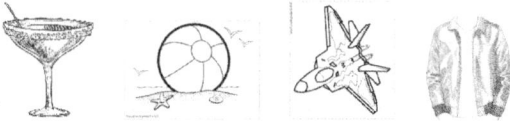

The nervous energy comes from knowing if I want to understand what took place at Champ's house, I will need to wake up my "gifts." Something I do not care to do.

It has been so pleasant not worrying about my psychic abilities running rampant the last few days. No voices in my head, no ghost sightings, and no weird dreams. I was not even getting visions from Wesley when we were holding hands.

It is like I am almost ordinary. Ordinary, in my book, is good.

I pull onto Champ's street and immediately see the green-and-white police cruiser sitting in the driveway. My heart sinks. It has taken two days to convince myself using my psychic abilities is something I must do. I can't guarantee I will persuade myself a second time.

"That is bad luck. What now?" Trisha asks.

"I don't know. I haven't gotten past this turn of events yet. I thought for sure everybody would be gone by now."

"They are down to one cruiser. At least the authorities don't seem to have all the crime scene technicians here now. Maybe they are planning on leaving soon."

"Maybe."

I'm afraid I have reached a dead end. I have a recording that does not confirm or deny anything. I can't get into Champ's house for the off-chance opportunity my psychic abilities can pull a reading and identify the actual killer.

If I could talk to Ace, it would help me put some of this together. But there is no logical excuse for me to get the opportunity to talk to Ace. Norman's friend, Stephen, has already gone out on the limb by getting me the surveillance recording, so I can't expect a second favor from there.

This is like the police cold cases. Once the opportunity for more information slows or comes to a halt, the only choice is to wait for an epiphany or an additional piece of information to fall into your lap.

"I was hoping we could get in, too. I want to put my hand on the front door and see if I get a weird feeling like I did at Ace's."

I am an idiot. That is the whole reason I thought of going to Champ's house to start. "Do you mind if we drive by Ace's? I would like to see if there is anything that looks out of place to me, too."

Trisha shrugs. "Sure. I'm not in any rush."

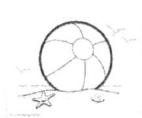

Chapter 14

Champ's house is a modest brick home in a well-established neighborhood with a mix of old and new construction. It is an upper-middle-income subdivision. Ace's apartment, situated on the north side of Pensacola, is even scarier during the day when I can see the condition of the neighborhood. The area has long gone to seed.

"I guess rent is cheap around here," Trisha says.

That remark will get her into the understatement of the year contest. We pull into the apartment complex's parking and have to avoid two monstrous potholes before finding an available slot.

I get out of the car. Trisha stays buckled in. "You are not coming with me?"

She shakes her head vehemently. "Oh, no. I already know there is something evil in that apartment. I don't want to accidentally anger it."

I know I should not stare at her, but that is rich. Especially considering if we angered something evil, Trisha would never see it chasing us.

With a mental eye roll, I shut my car door. I walk toward the apartment Ace entered the other night. I begin to put my hand to the door. Like magic, it opens. A man dressed in shorts and a three-quarter-sleeve T-shirt looks up, stopping just in time to avoid plowing into me. I take a step back as he draws up in surprise.

"Oh." He frowns. "Can I help you?"

"Hi. I'm Star from the Baker and Baker Development Agency." Talk about all the lousy luck in the world. What is the probability someone, most likely Ace's roommate Bart, would be leaving as I go to touch the door? "I'm canvassing the area to do a survey."

Bart's eyes make a creepy, slow trail up and down my body. "Survey for what?"

Right. What am I surveying? "Apartment preferences," I say, struggling to keep a straight face. "My client is considering building in the area and wants to know what amenities would be important to people who already rent in the area. Can you help me out?"

Bart grins as if I just told the most humorous joke. He stares pointedly at my breast as he answers. "I would love to help you out."

Yuck.

He shifts his weight, opening the door to the apartment wider. A glove and softball bat in his other hand come into my view.

His eyes shift to my legs. "The most important feature of an apartment to me is not having bugs. Last week I saw a cockroach that was so big it could win a tractor pull. The landlord tells me they spray, but I don't know."

"Bugs are the worst," I say.

"Aren't they."

"Say, I have not gotten to see any of the competing floor plans in the area. You don't suppose I could take a quick look around, do you?"

Bart sighs. "I'm supposed to be at softball practice in ten minutes." His eyes finally meet mine. "What the heck. We can do a quickie."

I step into the apartment. I am well aware every person in my extended family would be most upset with my carelessness.

"Excuse the mess. My roommate just moved out the other day. This apartment is a lot of space for one guy to take care of."

I step over a small pile of laundry randomly placed in the living room. I point to what must be a small galley kitchen. Do the oven and stove give even heat?"

"I couldn't tell you. I'm more of a microwave guy. You know—heat it up quick and eat it *slowly*."

I'm overcome by a queasy feeling. Bart's terrible double entendre is not the cause. It's that the apartment reeks of sweaty male underwear and greasy fast food long since spoiled. There is another smell, subtle, yet the scent has my mind spinning and my stomach churning. It is a copper smell like when I was a kid and held a handful of pennies on a sweltering day for too long.

"The room where all the magic takes place is over here."

I'm not sure what I thought I would find when I started this charade. Still, I will need to stay in character and see it through. I approach to give a cursory review of Bart's room.

The copper smell intensifies, and I feel nauseated. "Nice," I say as I step into the disgusting clutter.

I will need to spray Windex on the bottom of my shoes before getting into my car. "It's a two-bedroom?"

Bart steps back and lifts the glove and bat hand to his left. "Yeah. My roommate's room is across the hall."

"Do you mind if I take a look?"

Bart shrugs. "I guess not."

I walk past him in the doorway, and the coppery smell nearly bowls me over. It is coming directly from Bart.

"Dude is sort of weird," Bart says as he follows me.

"I just want to confirm the rooms are the same size." I open the door to a pristine room that could be mistaken for a shrine to naval aviation. Most prominently, the Blue Angels.

Bart is close behind me. The hair on the back of my neck stands up when he says, "He is not right. I didn't want to mention this, but he has not moved out. He is in jail."

"Jail!" I turn and do my best "I'm so horrified" face.

Bart appears encouraged. "Yep, murdered a dude in cold blood the other night."

Blood! That is what I am smelling. I search every inch of Bart since the smell seems to be emanating from him. There are no bloodstains on his clothes.

He stands taller as he notices I'm examining him closely. "This is sort of like we were supposed to meet. You and me, you know?"

Since I identified the smell, it's intensifying in strength. My head swirls, I feel faint, and my mouth begins to water as if I am close to vomiting. "I need to go." I push past Bart and the coagulating blood smell.

"Well, hey—wait—how do I get in touch with you?" Bart follows me to the front door.

"Don't be silly. I know where you live. I will just drop by."

My comment stops him at the door. Thank the Lord for small blessings.

"Okay," he says haltingly.

I take the concrete steps two at a time to the sidewalk drawing in deep breaths of fresh air as I go.

"Don't wait too long," Bart yells.

Only a lifetime, buddy.

Chapter 15

I have had about as much of "Mother Trisha" as I can stomach. She has been mean-mugging me and giving short, tight-lipped responses whenever I ask her a question.

The doorbell announces Wesley and Hank's arrival. It could not have come at a better time.

I don't care how upset Trisha is with me. I learned a lot from my little foray behind enemy lines. I have no idea what any of the information I gathered at Bart's means. Still, I know it is crucial to solving Champ's murder.

"You are in for a treat tonight," Wesley says, drawing my attention to him and his sexy face.

"Tell me about it." I put my hand on his hand that rests on the center console—because I can—and it makes me feel good.

"We have reservations for pier dining at The Lighthouse."

"Fancy." I am thoroughly impressed. The Lighthouse restaurant caters to an older—read, retired—wealthier clientele. Any reservations are tough to schedule. A reservation in their pier dining area is impossible.

"I have never gotten to sit there before," Trisha says.

"You know how to make a girl feel special, Lieutenant Greenwood," I say.

He smiles at me. "You are special, April."

Wesley is a fantastic catch himself—for some lucky girl. Not me, of course. I have my career dreams to stay focused on.

The Lighthouse sits on a prime piece of real estate on the Gulf Breeze side of the bay. The peninsula it is built on offers a clear view of the bay from three sides of the restaurant designed to look like an ancient antebellum mansion. The sun rests only a few feet from dipping into the water as we pull into the lot.

As Wesley hands the Jeep keys to the valet, I commit everything to memory. The light breeze lifting my hair off my shoulders while pushing my cotton dress against my legs. The sun reflecting off the bay, casting silver, orange, and gold rays across the landscape. The mild tang of salt on my lips and the incredibly hot man offering his arm to me.

I slip my arm into Wesley's as he leads me into the restaurant. A girl could get used to this really quickly.

"Did you have anything interesting happen today?"

I try to wipe the alarmed expression from my face. I am compelled to share the details of my meeting with Bart with Trisha. Still, I do not want to ruin this moment by having Wesley explain how foolish I was to enter the apartment alone. "Just another quiet day relaxing on the beach."

"That must be a tough life, but somebody has to live it," Wesley says with a grin.

Our table, incredibly, is at the edge of the short pier. It's as if our table and chairs are on the water.

The conversation between the four of us begins to elude me. My mind starts working overtime, attempting to solve the equation of my life events.

This is good. Being with Wesley feels right. I believe I want more of him in my life. The inconvenient truth is wanting and being able to do something are two vastly different things.

There is a chance all these feelings are me slowing down, finally living life, while becoming open to more than an occasional date. That is it. That makes all the sense in the world. I have been focusing on finishing school for so long that I never considered the whole dating idea the last few years. It was simply a novelty I could not afford.

Wesley laughs at something Trisha said and draws me back to the present long enough for me to stare at him and listen to his deep, baritone voice as he compliments her wit. I practically melt in my chair as I watch them interact. Lord, help me. I think I love this guy.

I can tell myself I feel all mushy inside because I have not been in a romance in years. But who am I kidding? It's not the newness of a date I am feeling. I want the man sitting with me tonight. The epiphany rocks me to my core. I let out a slight gasp.

The conversation stops. All three of my dinner partners stare at me. If I could, I would crawl under the table.

"Is everything all right?" Trisha asks me.

I dismissively wave my hand. "Hiccups."

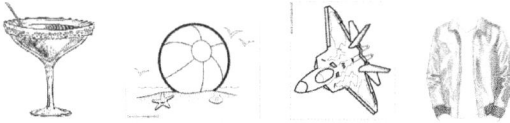

Wesley pulls his Jeep into the state park's lot. He turns the Jeep off, leaving the radio on. Jason Aldean sings to us about his girlfriend in cut-off jeans.

Hank opens his door. "Trisha and I are going for a walk."

I start to ask Trisha if she wants us to go with them and realize they are not going for a walk so much as getting out of our space. After my earlier epiphany, being alone with Wesley scares me.

I did not go to college for the last seven years to become a housewife. I know I am sort of putting the cart before the horse here—especially considering I have not even kissed Wesley. Still, I do feel like if we start down that road, it has a steep downhill grade. I will not have the willpower to fight for my dreams. Considering how hard I had struggled to get to this stage, throwing my dreams away for sexual urges is not acceptable.

Admittedly, they are not all sexual urges. They are just the ones bubbling to the top in an uber-urgent manner presently.

"I forget how many stars are in the sky until I get away from the city lights," Wesley says.

I want to say something witty and intelligent. All I can do is nod my head in agreement and hope he can see me in the dark.

"I'm glad you were able to go to dinner with us tonight. I really enjoyed it."

"I appreciate it. But I do hate that you and Hank picked up such an expensive meal. I would offer to cook you dinner tomorrow night to make up for it. But I'm afraid that would be adding insult to injury given my lack of cooking skill."

He chuckles as he rubs his forehead. "I love your honesty, April. It cracks me up."

Wesley is obviously defective. My honesty usually ticks people off. Rarely does it amuse.

We enjoy a few minutes of companionable silence. "Can I ask you something?" Wesley interrupts the quiet.

"Sure."

"When we asked you to go to dinner the day we met, what made you say yes? I mean before you took the emergency phone call."

"Trisha. She is a little awkward around guys. I could tell she was intrigued by Hank. I thought it would be a good opportunity for her to get comfortable with the idea of dating."

"Oh," Wesley says. He turns his head, looking out the driver's window.

"And I thought you were sexy."

He laughs again. "*Thought*?"

"Okay, *think*. Why? Do you have some sort of inferiority complex needing to be stroked?"

"No, but I do like hearing it. *From you*." He turns his head and locks eyes with me as his expression turns serious. "I did not intend for this to happen. I want you to know I don't expect anything from you—"

Every muscle in my body strains ridged as my skin tingles wildly. I am petrified at what Wesley will say next.

"But I do love you, April Snow."

Great. The cat is out of the bag *now*. You cannot put the toothpaste back in the tube once somebody releases the "L" word into the atmosphere.

I consider what Wesley professes as his lips suddenly press against mine. Electric shocks fly from my lips to my tailbone. Warm and soft, his lips feel divine on mine.

The pressure he exerts on my lips lessens. I feel him pull back. I place a hand on his shoulder and pull him closer to me.

His hand laces into the length of my hair, and his grip tightens. My lips part in surprise as he pulls me closer in a movement that speaks to a burning lust. His tongue teases my lower lip as all my brain functions shut down.

All there is, all there ever was, is the two of us in this embrace. This kiss is unlike any I have ever experienced. It is not a localized lip-to-lip contact. It's as if our energy fields have melded together and are surging between us.

I would be content if we could stay here like this forever.

"Let's get it on," Hank sings as he slides into the Jeep.

We break our kiss. Self-consciously I cover my lips.

"I see you kids are getting along," Trisha says as she pulls up into the Jeep.

"There is such a thing as knocking," Wesley grumbles.

"Well, hey. While we are talking about social norms. You could have put a sock on the door." Hank slaps Wesley on the shoulder. "Oh, wait. You don't have any socks on. My bad, bro."

Hank and Trisha devolve into a fit of laughter as Wesley starts the Jeep. He appears less than amused with Hank.

I'm right there with him.

It could be we are all tired, or there is too much sexual frustration in the Jeep. We remain silent on the ride home.

That is good by me. I have plenty to mull over.

If I thought I had a bad case of Wesley-itis earlier, the soul-binding kiss we shared only made it terminal. Now, once again, my brain is working overtime. I am trying to solve a problem with no probable solution. I want to be a partner at a big-time law firm. It will always be my goal to be the most sought-after defense attorney in the Southeast.

Unfortunately, Wesley's career—which he is equally passionate about and has spent years working toward—will require him to move from state to state regularly. Not to mention the nine-and-half-month deployments away from home, leaving his wife to take care of the house, children, and whatever else comes up by herself.

How do military wives do that?

There is no denying the facts as much as I want to bend them to my will—my heart. We cannot achieve our career goals simultaneously.

But maybe there is another way. Wesley could retire in twenty years. I'm twenty-seven now. Would forty-seven be too late to start my climb up the corporate ladder?

Strike that last comment. That is a crazy idea. Wesley has obviously kissed me plumb stupid.

Wesley drives the Jeep into our driveway. Trisha and Hank exit the Jeep and walk toward the front door.

I get out, and Wesley meets me at the front of the Jeep. He takes my hands in his, leans against the Jeep pulling me toward him until my legs are between his.

"I need to tell you something," he says.

My gut tenses, and I feel lightheaded. I don't know what I will do if Wesley tells me he wants me to be his fiancée and wait on him. At this moment, he could talk me into moving to Cleveland if that is where his next assignment is located. That is saying a lot for a Southern girl. I don't do winter weather.

I panic and hurry to beat him to the punch. "You do not have to say anything, Wesley."

He tilts his head to the right as he squints his eyes. "Well, I wouldn't want you to think we just abandoned you."

Now I'm confused. "Abandoned us?"

"Do you think you and Trisha can make an early lunch tomorrow? Hank and I have this thing tomorrow night. We will need to be back at the base early."

"Only if you let us buy."

"Please stop worrying about that. We live on base. There is not a whole lot for us to spend our cash on. It's not some hardship you have to be concerned about."

"I'm not worried about it. I just want to."

"Okay." He tilts his head back while studying my expression. "Sure. Thank you."

I pick at the bottom button on his golf shirt. "Don't thank me yet. I haven't told you where we are taking you."

"It does not matter to me. I would follow you anywhere, April."

Tears suddenly fill my eyes. My knees become so suspect I do not trust them not to unhinge. "Oh, aren't you so sweet—" I say, looking down before he lifts my chin with a finger placing his lips on mine. I'm lost in our kiss once again.

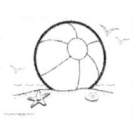

Chapter 16

I hit the play button again to watch the whole sixty-five-second recording to play. I'm trying to distract myself long enough to fall asleep. After Wesley's kiss, every cell in my body is electrified to a level of sexual expectation that can't possibly be healthy.

I don't believe I have ever been jonesing this bad for skin-on-skin action. Especially sexual activity that positively cannot lead to anything. Some nights I detest being a responsible, goal-oriented girl.

"You have got to stop obsessing about that recording, April," Trisha complains.

"Yeah, I'm obsessing. You forget an innocent man is sitting in jail right now. We may be the only two people who can help him."

Trisha scoffs. "I am sure they already appointed him a defense attorney. So, there is some help for him. Second, it does not matter how many times you watch the recording. It is still Ace walking around Champ's house minutes before he was brutally murdered. Case closed."

I shake my head. "No. This can't end this way." I stand as I shut my laptop.

As I slide my sandals on, Trisha sits up. She has an alarmed expression. "What are you doing?"

"Putting my shoes on so I can go see if the police left Champ's house yet. With any luck, I can sneak in and see if I can find any clues."

"You cannot just go in there."

"I can if the coast is clear. And I plan on it," I say.

Trisha throws the covers off. As she pulls on her tennis shoes, she preaches, "That whole talk I gave about the dangers of you going into Bart's apartment today is just in one ear and out the other?"

I roll my lower lip out as I shake my head. "Of course not. I listened. I'm just not going to take the advice to heart."

"Hold on then. You are not going by yourself," Trisha says.

"You don't need to go. I can do this on my own."

"Right. And would I be able to live with myself if something happens to you and you fail to come home?"

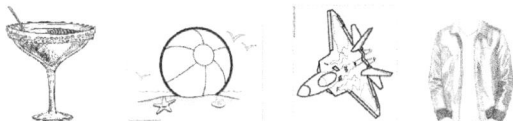

Butterflies circle in my stomach as we pull onto Champ's street. My luck is holding out as the only indication of police activity is a single yellow, plastic strip of police crime scene tape across the front porch. "Pull over here," I tell Trisha.

I scan up and down the street. It is as quiet as I expect it to be at 2:00 AM. I get out and make my way to the front door. It's locked up tight. I stand in the light of the porch for a few seconds, trying to decide if I should leave or continue trying to gain entry.

Finish what you start, April. You would not have come this far if you did not think it crucial.

Oh, alright. I stomp to the side of the house and try the first window. It slides halfway up with the slightest exertion from me.

I look behind me again. The street is still quiet. I give Trisha a thumbs up, then pull myself into the house via the window.

As I roll onto the floor, I wish I had thought to bring a flashlight with me. In lieu of that, I hit the flashlight function on my phone as a wave of nausea visits me. A starburst migraine stabs at the base of my skull.

Something nasty and mean either lives here or something terrible happened here recently.

I do some quick, deep breathing to steel my nerves and dull the sharpness of the pain.

I clear all the cluttering thoughts from my mind that do not pertain to the room. My brother Dusty refers to this mindset as "danger close focus." I have not the slightest clue what I just dropped into, but there is a cloying, oily feel to the air. The place smells like a porta-potty at a Fourth of July free fish fry. I must stay alert in case I need to make a quick retreat.

Standing, I do a brief search of the room with my phone's flashlight while I let the last of the migraine subside. A desk with a laptop on top and a safe tucked underneath clue me in that this is Champ's home office.

True to Detective Keaton's word—who claimed Champ was a local high school sports stud—dozens of football and basketball trophies line a long shelf to my left. If Champ is still on this plane, and given the abrupt and violent nature of his death, it would be my bet that a place such as his office would be a probable spot for his ghost to occupy.

Like the coward I am, I consider rolling back out the window and calling it a night. The excrement stench alone is enough to let me know I have no business messing around with whatever is wrong with this house.

After I stare at the open window mocking me for a moment, and my heart rate regulates to normal, I decide not to run. Please, do not credit me for being a hero who wants to free an unjustly accused man. My hyper curiosity is all that is driving my determination.

Now that I am in the house and my nerves have somewhat calmed, I wonder if Champ's ghost is still here. The negative energy seems too elevated to be pure residual emotions.

I stand in the middle of the room and focus. Bringing all of my energies inward, I compact them as tightly as possible at my sternum. Once I am calm, I push my power outward as I search for anything of a paranormal nature.

As the rush of the mental exercise cools, I can't help but be disappointed. It seemed like such a logical place for Champ's spirit to reside. The only thing present in the room is an incredibly pronounced essence of negativity laced with vanity and coercion. I am sure this was a pleasant place to call home.

I am mildly bummed Champ no longer dwells on this side of the veil. So much for easy identification of his actual killer. I figure I did the hard part by gaining access. I might as well check out the rest of the house. There is a chance I may find something that will clue me in or be of use later.

I enter what I assume to be the living room. My eyes play tricks on me as I note a quick motion in the shadows to my left. I swing my phone's light in that direction. Nothing.

Get it together, April.

The living room shares the putrid smell of the office. Still, there is another scent now mingling with the poop smell. A sickly-sweet-smelling woman's perfume. A perfume that has sat forgotten at the back of someone's vanity and long since spoiled.

The attitude of the room has also changed. Bitterness and manipulation are added to the coercion.

This place is a mood nightmare. Unfortunately, like rubbernecking an accident, I am now more invested than ever at finding out every little detail of this house. April just stepped over the "this is scaring the bejesus out of me" line to "my goodness, what else will I find?"

Hyper curiosity is a dangerous trait.

Like in Champ's office, I clear my thoughts of all except the task at hand. I focus my energies on my core. This time I'm not surprised when my senses come back as a big zero. Nothing remains except a lot of leftover nastiness hanging in the air and on the walls.

I turn my attention to the kitchen, complete with two sinks, two ovens, and a beautiful center island done in a handsome dark-gray granite. I squash the tiny flame of envy igniting in my belly as I picture my dinky kitchen in my Tuscaloosa apartment.

There is barely a whisper of energy in the kitchen. Other than the microwave, nobody ever came in here. Meh—on second thought, their kitchen is a lot like mine, after all.

I look across the living room to the hallway. I assume it leads to the bedrooms. A grin stretches across my face as I whisper, "Oh, yeah. Let's see what is going on in the bedroom." So, sue me. I have a bit of a voyeuristic streak.

My heart rate peaks as I reach the hallway. Unlike my parents' home, I note there is not a single picture in the hall. That does not surprise me. This was not exactly a loving home.

A sudden twinge tweaks my insides, and I stop. Random.

I consider the doors in front of me. This seems odd since I plan to check the entire house anyway. Just start by going into the nearest room. Right?

A closed room is at the end of the hallway. Two doors are on my right and one on the left. Eeny, meeny, miny, moe, master bedroom on the left.

I sense a strong current pulling me to the door. Of course, I do. Any overly curious voyeur knows the master bedroom will be chock full of juicy emotions to complete the portfolio of this house of dysfunctional horrors.

I am not disappointed. As I clear the threshold, the other emotions pale as lust becomes the predominant motivation in the air. The salty-sweet smell of lovers' sweat wafts through the air.

My mind wanders to the kiss Wesley and I shared earlier. If Trisha and Hank had not been with us, I know we would have left some thick lust energies and the scent of lovers' sweat in Wesley's Jeep.

Too bad Wesley is not a psychic. That would have been humorous. To leave something behind, so every time Wesley gets in his Jeep, he remembers our mad lovemaking session. Which, of course, never happened. It only lives as a figment of my imagination.

I continue further into the master bedroom while visions of Wesley and me wrestling naked in the back of his Jeep play through my mind. The mattress is missing from the box springs against the far wall.

That makes sense to me, regardless of who killed Champ. Champ was a big guy, and from all the sports accolades, I would assume a rather good athlete. Not exactly the type of person you want to take on in hand-to-hand combat. Whoever killed him surprised him in his sleep.

I lean over to take a closer inspection of where Champ's head would be while he slept. There is no bullet hole in the box springs. Perhaps the missing mattress had enough mass to retain the two rounds. Since forensics either took the bed or the police disposed of it as a biohazard, I will never know.

I check the wall for bullet holes in case the killer fired my gun at a steep angle and a round went undetected. The wall could use a paint job, but there are no holes. Still, I lean in closer. The wall is speckled like a robin's egg. Except the tiny, ruddy speckles are on dingy white drywall rather than the pretty shade of blue.

Leaning even closer, my mind spins with the meaning of blood spatter on the wall. It does not seem likely that a forty-five slug to the head would make a light pattern like this.

If Champ were close enough to the wall for his blood to end up here, and my gun was used, I would expect to see evidence of a massive mess cleaned by the biohazard team. Or if he was too far away, nothing at all. This appears more like a blunt object spatter to me.

A sudden rage courses through me, but it is not my anger. The attitude of the room has shifted dramatically.

I catch a cold draft across my left cheek as I stand straight. It makes me jerk and turn. As I do, I accidentally smack the back of my left leg against the bed. I lose my balance and fall backward onto the box spring.

From my prone vantage point, I see the dark, diesel-like smoke collecting in the corner of the ceiling. *Darn it, April. You let yourself get distracted!*

The quickest way out of the room is to sit up and run to the bedroom door. Still, as the smoke snakes down in a thin, spiraling column nearly touching the floor, I begin to crab crawl back across the box spring. As I reach the opposite edge of the bed, the smoke expands and transforms into a roughhewn humanoid shape.

"You!" The word booms inside my head.

I roll off the bed onto my feet and start toward the bedroom door to make my escape. Angry Smoke Man slides across the room in a tenth of a second, blocking the door from me.

Forced to stop or plow through the entity, I consider my other alternatives. A three-foot-long portion of the column swings out from the humanoid shape, striking me across the face. I yelp and fall back to get away. The taste of blood springs into my mouth.

I scramble to my feet. Standing on the box springs, I scream at the spirit, "Stop it, or I will leave!"

The humanoid shape floats to within an inch of my face. Slowly, what would be the head of the spirit forms in more detail, allowing me to see the calculating, coal-black eyes in the dark fog in front of me.

I am so scared I can't trust my knees not to unhinge and drop me on my butt. "We can help each other, or I can leave. Your choice."

Champ's ghost does not slap me again. I take that as a truce. "The police have charged Ace Gilbert with your murder," I begin.

"Where is he? I will kill the little coward." Champ's angry voice echoes in my head. "The police station. He has to be." The ghost begins to slide through the bedroom door.

"Wait." What remains of Champ stops moving through the door but does not turn. "So, Ace *did* kill you?"

There is no voice in my head. Champ floats back into the room. The anger which fills the room so wholly loses its sharp edge.

"I understand you are angry. I'm sure I would be too. I am hoping Ace did not kill you. That it was someone else. Some details about your case do not add up, Champ."

Champ's ghost loses its humanoid shape, turning back into a thick column. I wait for the voice in my head, but again there is nothing. "Please. I must know for my own peace of mind. Was Ace your killer, or was it someone else?"

"Somebody has to pay. I do not like Ace—and now that I think about it—I do not like you, either." The voice grumbles in my head, and I nearly pee myself.

Still, Champ's words clear things up immensely. "You didn't see your killer. Did you?"

"I was asleep."

Then there is a possibility Ace did not kill Champ. Now I need to find someone who had a motive as good or better than Ace's. Someone who was also in the area of Champ's house the night of the murder.

"I'm working to identify who killed you, Champ."

The smoky column's hands become more detailed, and the black eyes appear once again approximately where Champ's head should be. I feel the malice building in the smoke and sense I am running out of time.

"I think I will kill you. Then I will pay Ace a visit in his jail cell."

I'm not gonna say my whole life flashes in front of me. Still, his words render me discouraged that I will never see my family again.

And that I spent so many years busting my butt in school just for the police to find me strangled to death in a house that was the sight of a homicide three days earlier. Boy, won't that be a talked-about headline in my hometown paper?

"Listen, I am convinced Ace was framed for your murder. Let me remind you. If Ace was set up, that means somebody planned to murder you. Planned it for a long time.

"I get you do not like me. But in the interest of finding out who betrayed you, wouldn't it be worth letting Ace and me live if I could identify your real killer?"

The column undulates in front of me for what seems like an eternity. Long streamers of smoke float through the ceiling above. As the last tendrils of inky black disappear, I hear in my head. "You have twenty-four hours. Don't disappoint me."

I shut the car door the second I hop into my seat. Trisha eyes me as I buckle my seatbelt.

"What happened to your face?" she asks.

"I bumped into a piece of furniture when I crawled through the window," I lie.

Trisha studies me for a second, then starts the car. "Okay. In the interest of keeping the peace, I will let that slide. Did you find anything inside?"

"Nothing helpful." And that *is* the truth. All I found was a ticked-off ghost who couldn't even tell me who killed him. What a bust.

Chapter 17

The following day, I am on the beach trying my best not to think about Ace. I have done everything I can do. Which is more than most people have done to prove his innocence.

I still do not believe Ace killed Champ. Still, I need to resolve myself to the facts. The circumstantial evidence the police have is insurmountable. He will be found guilty. There is nothing his defense attorney nor I can do to change that outcome.

Selfishly, the whole incident irks me to no end. Between the readings I felt at Bart's apartment and the conversation with Champ's ghost, there is a real chance my psychic abilities will snap to life again. And for what? I have increased the likelihood of my "gifts" coming back to life with a vengeance without accomplishing anything in return.

All those things are rearview mirror items. There is no reason to spend any more time worrying or fretting about them. I can't fix them. What is done is done. All I can do now is move forward with a positive attitude.

And why should I not be optimistic? I am on a beautiful beach with my favorite cousin, and the sexiest guy I have ever known will call and let me take him to lunch in fifteen minutes.

Who knows, maybe I will even offer Wesley some "dessert" today. I feel a little wild, and the other night in the Jeep left me hungry for something sweet.

"Should they have called already?" Trisha asks.

I stand and shake out my beach towel. "The boys will not be late. They still have a few minutes."

Like magic, my phone rings. I smile when I see "Wesley" on the screen. "Hey, are you here?"

"Yes, we just pulled into the lot. Do you need some help with your beach gear?"

"Nope. We will be there in a minute." I hang up and take down our umbrella. "They are here," I tell Trisha.

As we pack our gear, I have a nagging sense that Wesley's voice sounded different this morning. Of course, this is the first time I have talked to him on the phone down by the beach. I'm sure it is only the noise of the water that made him sound different.

Trudging up the long, weathered-wood ramp, I spot both men sitting on the railing by the shower. As we approach, they hop down.

"If you give us the key to your car, we can pack your beach gear while you rinse off," Wesley offers.

"That's sweet of you," I say. Trisha digs her keys out of our bag and hands them our bag and umbrella.

I watch the two men walk toward our car as I turn the shower on. "Do they seem like they are acting sketchy?" I ask.

Trisha looks in their direction. She turns to rinse her hair. "Maybe. I mean, Hank is such a horndog. I would have expected him to want to watch us shower."

I bark a laugh. "Did you just call your boyfriend a horndog?"

Trisha flashes a full smile. "He is a perv. And he is not my boyfriend."

"Then, what is he?"

She shrugs again. "I don't know. I haven't figured that out just yet."

Leave it to Trisha to surprise me. Here I was worried she might fall in love, and she is the one who has kept it all easy breezy.

Me? I am afraid I have fallen hard for Lieutenant Wesley Greenwood. I am not sure how we fit our lives together. But I have almost convinced myself it's worth working out all those pesky details, like two demanding careers and how we will work out living in two different cities.

CJ's, the restaurant Trisha and I take the boys to, is located by the Fisherman's Wharf. It continually smells of stale beer and fish guts. Still, the fish is usually from that day's charters. The freshness makes it unlike any fish you have eaten.

Wesley orders the fried Spanish mackerel. I select the grilled yellowfin tuna. We share so much off each other's plates it might as well be a family combo.

I know the food is delicious. Still, it could be fish sticks and it would be fine. Sitting with Wesley chatting about our morning is just so intimate. Most of all, it seems normal.

I know it is sad, but "normal" is the state I aspire to the most. If I could just be rid of my "gifts" and settle into a routine with a man I love. That would be the most enjoyable situation.

Wesley takes my hands in his. "Okay. There is something I need to tell you."

Hank grimaces across the table. "Man, do we really have to do this right now?"

"Yes, it is important."

My stomach tightens as my mind races to think about what Wesley could ask me that is so important. My heart rate races out of control as a thought comes to mind. Surely he is not going to ask that.

What would I say? Lord, I am hyperventilating.

Calm it, April. We have just started seeing each other.

But possibly—just maybe—he feels the same way I do and wants to make this a more permanent part of his life, too.

Wesley looks down as he starts to talk. "April, these last few days have been absolute heaven. I genuinely care for you. But you know Hank and I are here for flight training. It has just been a co-incidence our schedules dovetailed so well the last few days."

I can't tell where this is going. The smile on my face feels increasingly fake the longer Wesley talks. He needs to make his point—and soon.

"But one of the exercises we have to complete is our survival training. It is a two-week program where we are in the field the entire time."

My head is bobbing up and down like an idiot. I have the gut feeling Wesley is attempting to tell me something I will not like. Still, I'm not comprehending.

"Tonight, we leave for the exercise. We return in two weeks."

"But I will be gone in two weeks," I protest.

Wesley nods his head. "I know. That is why I'm telling you now. I'm sorry."

My nose tingles and my eyes burn—which angers me. "You are telling me I won't see you again?"

"Not until we plan something after you get settled in Atlanta, and I finish flight school."

Wesley's eyes meet mine, and I can see he is doing his best to be positive and make it all good.

But it's not.

It's complete and utter rubbish.

How can he leave me when we are having such an enjoyable time? This could be the romance of a lifetime for him, and he is going? I don't understand. I mean, I do, stupid airplanes—no, helicopters. Oh, who cares? Doesn't he feel this? Did I convince myself he felt this, too? Oh, bless it. What sort of a fool have I been?

"But I thought we were having a good time?" I hear my voice plead. I hate myself for the desperate words.

He squeezes my hands. "Beyond a good time. The best of times. I have never connected with anyone like I have connected with you these past days."

"But you're leaving."

He chokes back a nervous laugh. "It's just the job, April. It's got nothing to do with you and me."

But it does. It has *everything* to do with the two of us. This is the scenario I played over and over in my head. This has driven me crazy the last two days ever since I realized my heart went to Wesley Greenwood without my permission.

Whether I want to admit it or not, this is how I always knew our relationship would end. It was inevitable, and I refused to accept the fact. I'm feeling angry and a lot bitter.

Fine, I'm a truckload of bitter.

Even though I know it is ungrateful, I can't be big enough to be thankful for the fun time we spent together.

"Say something, April. Please," Wesley begs.

I pull my hands from him and turn my head, worried I am about to devolve into a full-fledged, snot-filled cry. He will *not* see me cry. He is not worth that. "I think I want to go home."

"We can plan to get together in a few weeks, April."

"Take me home now, please," I croak.

"Go ahead and give her a ride home, Wesley. Trisha and I will call for a ride. We want to take a walk on the beach," Hank says.

Trisha lays her hand on mine. "Are you okay?"

I hop off the barstool. "Never been better." I take a few steps away from the table and wait for Wesley to follow.

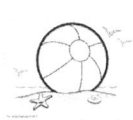

Chapter 18

We get in the Jeep without a word. Wesley starts across the Bay Bridge, and I stare out the window at all the boats and Wave-Runners out today. They are all out there having a blast. I'm riding in a Jeep with a broken heart.

Shame on me. I knew how this would end when I began playing with the fire. I have only myself to blame. I am a foolish, foolish girl.

"Can we not talk?"

"There is nothing left to talk about," I say harsher than I intend as my bitterness flows out.

Wesley's heavy sigh almost draws my eyes away from the happy people in the boats. I will not give him the satisfaction. "April, it's not like I hid my career from you. I was honest from the start. Military life can be difficult for spouses."

"Yep. You were perfectly honest, Wesley. You did not do anything wrong. It's just the job. It's got nothing to do with you and me. Got it. Roger Wilco and out, Lieutenant."

"Listen, I know you're hurting. For that, I am sorry, April. I never meant to hurt you."

A tear streaks down my right cheek. I suck in a deep breath and will the rest of my tears to stop. "It's got nothing to do with you. It's me."

"I—" Wesley is smart enough to know my statement is not

something I can explain, and he holds his question.

Darn it. I love that he knows there are times to talk things out and times to just be quiet.

Another tear rolls down my cheek, and the rest threaten to follow. I am disgusted with myself for being so emotional. We have only known each other for a few days. It is not like this is some six-year relationship falling apart.

But it hurts to the bone.

Riding in silence helps my attitude. As we reach the tollbooths on the Ocean Breeze side, my tears have stopped threatening to fall.

Be a big girl about it, April.

There are plenty of reasons for me to have a grateful heart. For a few days, I had a fantastic distraction. I mostly forgot about the terrible events from before I came to Pensacola. That is a good thing.

Plus, there are no pesky, complicating strings to mess up my master plan. I can now focus my full attention on being the best defense attorney in the Southeast. I could not do that if Wesley had fallen madly in love with me and pleaded for me to follow him all over the world while he flew helicopters and I stayed home with the kids. I never could have been happy with that life.

Anyway, this was just a summer fling thing. I mean, let's face it. Wesley is an absolutely gorgeous man and incredibly easy to be around. Still, as I noticed from the start, I would not be able to wear any heels over two inches at social gatherings. I do like to wear high heels to parties.

Ha, Trisha is so right. These flyboys were just something fun to pass the time and stroke our female egos.

Great, am I taking my dating cues from Trisha now? That is a little disconcerting, to say the least.

Maybe this once Trisha does have the right of it. If I had treated Wesley as a summer fling from the start, my heart never would have fallen so hard. There is nothing to be done about the pain now. It is like I get the foul-tasting medicine of a broken heart, but not the cookie of the sexual interaction to take away the bitterness. That bites.

Wesley pulls his Jeep into our driveway. He puts the truck in park, and my mind whirls with a kaleidoscope of random thoughts.

This is over. There is no way Wesley and I will get back together after he finishes his flight training. Parting lovers usually say they will meet up later and never do.

What would be the harm? People hook up all the time. Why not Wesley and me?

Not some grand last goodbye of an almost long-term relationship, just a simple hook up of two young people who find each other attractive and decide to have sex one night. What would be the harm in that?

Are you freaking kidding me? It will take weeks, if not months, to get over him as it is now. Throw a hot session of lovemaking on top of my emotions, and I might never get Wesley Greenwood out of my head.

Still, he could be a complete dud in bed. If there are no fireworks—or at least no fireworks for *me*—wouldn't that make it incredibly easy to put Wesley in my rearview mirror?

It would. That would be extremely helpful.

I know, you think I am just trying to justify a reason to get him in the sack before he leaves.

I'm too conflicted to make a rational decision. I do the mature thing. I decide if Wesley stays in the Jeep, it was never meant to happen. Then it is goodbye forever, my dear, sweet, thoughtful man. But if he follows me to the door, I will strip him buck naked and take advantage of him until he screams for mercy.

I pop open the Jeep door and close it behind me. I try to act nonchalant, which is difficult to do as my entire body is thrumming with nervous energy. I hear his door open, and I nearly trip on the stair leading to the front door. I pause at the door, sensing him at my back.

"I know you are angry. And I guess I get it. But please remember I am equally disappointed."

Turning, I try to determine the best method of grabbing hold of him to pull him into the condo without making a fool of my-self by getting us tangled up and falling onto the floor. The prob-lem is he won't quit talking.

"This is awful timing, April. If I had a few weeks more with you, I know I could convince you to come with me. Come see the world and be my life companion."

That little fire—which was stoking in my belly—a bucket of water just splashed across it. The sad thing is I have my answer. Wesley is thinking about the long game, too. The only thing is, in his mind, he figured it out by me abdicating my lifetime goals.

I stare into his beautiful golden-hazel eyes for what I now understand to be the last time. A girl is going to love waking up to that face every morning. It's just not going to be this girl.

"You are a strong, independent woman. You are tailor-made for being an officer's—"

I snatch the back of Wesley's hair and crush his mouth to mine. With total abandon, I take everything I can from him. When I release him, I take pleasure in noticing how shaken he is from the passion.

"Good luck with your survival test, Wesley."

Before he can say a word, and before I can change my mind, I slip into the condo and shut the door behind me. I know I have done the right thing for both of us. Still, a lot of times, the right thing does not feel good.

Right now, it hurts so badly I'm not sure I can take my next breath.

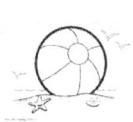

Chapter 19

If there has ever been a day I have been pissier, I cannot recall it. It is not my fault. Not a single thing has gone right today.

We were out of coffee this morning. The thong on my favorite pair of flip-flops broke. I have put on five pounds of bloat overnight. Adding insult to injury, the wind is so fierce, the top layer of my skin feels like it has been exfoliated by a sandblaster.

On the positive—well, there is no positive, except Trisha is still extremely happy, which means she probably did what I lost the nerve to do.

But I am not about to give her the satisfaction of telling me about it, so I have not asked her to share.

Man, the beach is blistering hot today. It's incredibly uncomfortable. "I'm going to go for a walk. Do you want to come along?"

Trisha keeps her eyes plastered to her Kindle. I know she is not reading it because she has not flipped a page in five minutes. She is just avoiding me.

"No, thank you. This book is getting to the good part."

Fine. I didn't feel like company anyway. I put my hat on in addition to my sunglasses. "I'm walking toward the pier side of the beach. I should be back in an hour."

"Okay. Have fun."

Have fun. As if.

Sweat rivulets run down my back at a furious pace. I consider a swim to cool off. Still, if I get in the water, I will end up with salt and sand in between my legs and start a friction fire. That would force me to sleep with my legs apart for a few days until the rash dies down. Darned if you do, darned if you don't.

Lord, I can hardly stand myself. If I can't snap out of this, I plan to walk into the ocean and drown myself like in one of those old-timey movies. Not really. It seems like that would be a horrible way to go. Not to mention how do you not try to swim once you start drowning?

It was the right decision. I keep telling myself that in the hope I will somehow believe myself someday. Today, all I can do is second-guess my choice and make everybody around me miserable.

Do you know what else makes me cranky? Seeing all these couples—high school, college, young parents, even geriatrics—walking around hand in hand or lying side-by-side having a fun time together on the beach.

Why them? Why do they get to be happy? Why do I have to have the impossible love life?

I know it is not some genetic disposition. My parents have been married thirty-some-odd years, and if they were here at the beach, they would be one of those couples irritating the stew out of me today.

Just look at the yahoos over there. I mean, can you get any more exhibitionist and not be at a nude beach? She calls that a swimsuit? I call it six feet of pink twine and three small jean patches. Look at the guy who is slathering lotion all over her. He is practically drooling on her shoulders.

I stop in front of them and realize I am beginning to gawk. Swiveling, I turn my view toward the water while I process that those two people look awfully familiar. Remarkably familiar, but not.

Nonchalantly, I act like I am looking for shells as I look back at the couple in my peripheral vision. I know that shade of red hair and am surprised I did not recognize Audrey straight off.

It shocks me a widow of three days would be out on the beach.

That is not fair of me. I suppose everybody grieves differently. Still, I think it's safe to say most people would think it's a little early for another man to be lathering her down with baby oil. Not to be judgmental, mind you.

Picking up shells and collecting them in my left hand to add credence to the "I'm just a little old shell hunter" act, I struggle to identify the lucky man. At first blush, he looks like Ace. Then I'm able to place his face. Bart, Ace's roommate.

The epiphany hits me hard. Oh no, Audrey is the married woman Bart is dating. Now that makes this a small awkward world to the point of ridiculous.

Yuck. Bart can't just apply lotion to Audrey. He gives her a full-body massage as if he is some beachside cabana boy masseuse. Still, it looks like it feels good.

I realize I'm staring, but something has caught my eye. As I watch Bart knead Audrey's flesh with his strong hands, my attention is drawn to his knuckles. His evenly tanned knuckles. And then everything clicks into place.

I try not to draw attention to myself to the best of my abilities, but I'm in a full out jog when I get back to Trisha. "Trisha, pack up. We have got to go."

She gives me a droll stare over the top of her Kindle. "Can't you relax for a minute?"

I scoop up my towel close the umbrella. "Seriously. We have got to go. I will explain in the car."

She starts to ask me a question. Instead, she stands and collects her things. Trudging through the sand toward our car, I look over my shoulder to make sure she is following me. She is just a few steps behind. "Skip the shower. I will clean your dad's car later."

I see her forehead wrinkle in question, but again she holds her tongue and continues to follow me. We sling our beach gear into the trunk. Trisha gets in and starts the car before asking, "Where to?"

At this point, I am ninety-five percent sure of my theory. Still, one of the things I learned in law school is ninety-five percent is not even close to being enough.

"We must go by the condo first. I need to check something out."

Trisha pulls out of the state park lot before she says, "Okay, now explain."

"Ace's roommate is dating Champ's widow."

Trisha whips her face in my direction. "Come again?"

I point at the windshield. "Watch the road."

She concentrates on driving for a moment before saying, "Well, that's *not* odd."

"I know, right?"

"So, what are we checking?"

I smile at her choice of the word "we." "Do you remember the tattoo on Ace's knuckles?"

"Need 4 speed."

"Exactly."

Trisha keeps her eyes on the road and raises her eyebrows. "And?"

"And Ace's roommate, Bart, does not have any tattoos on his knuckles."

Trisha's eyes squint as she appears to be processing the information. "That dirty snake. Why would he do that?"

"It is obvious why he might kill Champ. He acts like Audrey is the reincarnation of Aphrodite. I can understand framing someone, too. What good is freeing Audrey from her marital bond if you are in jail? But framing your roommate? That seems awfully cold."

Trisha guffaws. "You do know that you said it is cold to frame your roommate but didn't mention how cold you must be to murder somebody in their sleep."

"I'm just saying Champ would have been his adversary. He lived with Ace. They were supposed to be friends."

"But Bart might see Ace as a nerd." Trisha shakes her head. "People think it is okay to dump on nerds all the time."

I notice Trisha's jaw muscle flex. I am not touching the "nerd" conversation with a twenty-foot pole. Besides, I only have one focus right now. That is to confirm or disprove my hypothesis.

Trisha's nerd projection issues will have to wait.

We are both out of the car as soon as it stops at the condo. We race into our room and fire up my laptop.

As the recording plays, butterflies take flight in my stomach. I scan the man's left hand and see the knuckles are void of markings as the suspect walks on the sidewalk. I confirm the right knuckles are also void of ink when he grabs the doorknob.

"How did we miss that?"

"Too much eye candy," I say. "We had the jacket, hat, sunglasses, and face. That is way too many things to observe all at once. It really does not surprise me."

"I feel like such a failure." Trisha pokes her lower lip out.

"I missed it, too, and I don't feel like a failure."

"What do we do now?"

"Where is your dad?"

"He is in Panama City with some friends today."

That is not going to work for me. "If we call your dad, he will be at least two hours getting here. I'm not positive Audrey or Bart didn't see me. If they did and we are waiting here, we will be sitting ducks."

Trisha's eyes open wider. "Are you serious? You think they would come after us?"

"If you thought it meant the difference between fifty years in jail or getting away with something—what would you do?"

"You are scaring me."

I nod my head as I scoop up my laptop and take the keys out of Trisha's hands. "That is not necessarily unhelpful. Come on. Let's go to the police station and talk to your dad's friend, Stephen. Maybe he can help. At the very least, we can wait there for your dad after you call him."

Chapter 20

Stephen is not even humoring us anymore when Norman enters the station. I have been trying to explain to Stephen that Bart is who we see on the surveillance recording as I play it repeatedly on my laptop.

The tattoos on the knuckles, Stephen explains away. He believes Ace would realize them as identifying marks. Ace simply applied heavy stage makeup on his knuckles, according to Stephen.

I bring up the fact Ace would not wear sunglasses, a hat, and a jacket everybody had seen him wearing that night if he was trying to disguise himself. Stephen explains this away as anybody can buy the same gear online. He believes Ace knew it would not incriminate him.

I find the last bit particularly rich. The perpetrator wearing Ace's clothes is *precisely* why the police pushed Ace to the top of the persons of interest list. After viewing the recording, they were convinced they had their man.

Stephen reminds me Ace had a motive because of the fight earlier that night. More importantly, Ace had access to my gun, and the gunshot residue proved he fired it. I can't help but feel Stephen is trying to admonish me once again for my handling of the now infamous two shooter.

"But Bart has been dating Champ's wife. Isn't that motive?"

Stephen tilts his head to the right. "It could be, but it's not as strong of a motive as just having got your face kicked in by the man."

Trisha fills Norman in on the details as they walk into Stephen's office. I expect Norman can help move the conversation along and bring Stephen to understand his error.

"I'm sorry, Stephen." Norman turns to me. "I wish you girls called me before you came down here to bug Detective Lanham."

I am stunned by Norman's comment. "Did Trisha tell you about his hands? And about Bart and Audrey?"

"Yes, but the fact we can't see the tattoos does not make Ace innocent. And who Audrey dates is her business. She is a grown woman."

My jaw drops. It takes me a moment to respond. "The killer does not have tattoos," I say, extremely slowly and deliberately.

"Norman, I tried to explain to your girls it could just be makeup. Heck, we didn't find any fingerprints. Ace may be wearing gloves."

"There are no gloves. I can see the hairs on the back of his hand." Both men look at me like I'm crazy since I said that louder than intended.

Stephen raises his hands in a "calm down" gesture. "Understand, I am not saying I do not believe you. What I am saying is that unless we have something more compelling about Bart, Ace remains our target of the investigation."

Ace has really painted himself into a corner on this one. How he could have ticked off Audrey's husband enough to earn a butt-kicking on the very night Champ is killed is unfathomable. Me winning the Powerball is a surer bet than all those events occurring coincidentally.

Champ is killed with my gun, and Ace conveniently has gunshot residue on his hand from the shooting range the previous weekend. There is no way to prove anyone other than Ace and I had access to the murder weapon.

Wait. The murder weapon was not my gun. My forty-five was the coup de grâce. The red herring at the murder.

"If Bart possessed the murder weapon, would that be enough to convince you he is your culprit?" I ask.

Stephen glares at me and licks his lips. "What are you talking about."

"I'm talking about the real murder weapon. The one that killed Champ."

Norman squeezes my arm. "April, maybe we should discuss this with a lawyer before you say anything else."

I lay my hand on his hand. "No. We are good."

Norman lets go of my arm, but his expression is full of concern. I turn back to Stephen. "Champ was not killed with my gun. Was he?"

"Your gun was at the scene, and both bullets were spent."

I grin. "But that is not what killed Champ. *Is it*?"

"I can't reveal details of an ongoing investigation."

"What if I were to tell you Bart has a softball bat. I'm convinced if you spray his bat with Luminol, you will find blood traces. Specifically, blood traces from Champ."

Stephen's eyes narrow. "How do you know this?"

"I don't. It is just a theory. The question is, can you afford to ignore it."

Stephen glares at me as he picks up his radio. He points the radio antenna at me. "You better not be messing with me."

I think back to the blood smell I sensed when Bart was close by his softball bat while I investigated their apartment. I can still see the speckled cast-off pattern of blood on Champ's bedroom wall. I am only ninety-five percent sure I am right, But in this case, I will have to roll with the ninety-five percent and hope the last bit of evidence falls into place.

"No, sir. I'm positive."

"Okay. We will check it out," Stephen says as he leaves the office.

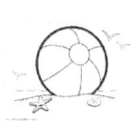

Chapter 21

Norman insists on a taco night celebration. As he puts it, "for his smart girls cracking the case open."

Since we have not received confirmation from Stephen yet, it seems premature. If I were to guess, Norman is simply tired of fish again and wants to cook something for us.

By the time we have completed our grocery shopping, it's nine o'clock. This is going to be a late dinner.

While Trisha and I watch Norman cook from the vantage of our high-backed stools, I have a horrible vision in my mind's eye. It scares me to the core.

"I will be back in a minute," I tell Trisha and walk out onto the back patio.

I start to dial him twice before I lose my nerve and consider how stupid it is. How do you explain a gut feel?

Don't be a chicken about this April. You will hate yourself if you don't say anything.

I resolve to call Wesley even if he thinks I am crazy. Heck, I probably am crazy.

"Hello?"

Despite the seriousness of what I have seen in my mind, his voice brings a smile to my face. "So, you are not out in the woods eating bugs yet, I take it?"

"No. All the crickets and wood cockroaches are safe for another hour or two."

"I'm going to ask this only once. If you say no, I understand. Still, I have to ask you."

"Okay," his voice is full of questions.

"Rather than me follow you all over the world, why don't you come to Atlanta with me? I'm sure you can eventually get on with an airline there. It is a huge hub. That way, you get the best of both worlds. You get to fly, and you get to stay with me."

There is a long pause. I know the answer before Wesley says, "April, I really wish I could. But understand I have wanted to fly helicopters for my country since I was a little boy. As much as I want to be with you, I don't want to miss out on my dream and maybe be resentful about it when I'm older."

Fair.

Not at all what I want to hear, but not totally unexpected, either. But I'm the one hung with a vision that may or may not be factual. You can't ever count on visions, but you can't discount them, either.

"Please reconsider. I do not want you to be in danger."

"Danger?" He laughs. "Baby, I could get killed tonight crossing the street. Besides, the United States has the best training in the world for aviators. There is nothing to worry about."

Well, that's that. "If you change your mind, the offer stands."

"Mine does too, April. Listen, I've got to go. I promise you I'll see you when I finish flight school and you are settled in Atlanta."

"Take care, Wesley."

"You too, April."

I disconnect the line and stare at my phone. I'm sure my vision was just a stupid reaction to all the stress of the day. I should not have bothered him with it. It sounds like he is swamped getting ready for his survival training.

The door opens, and Trisha says, "Stephen has stopped by. He says he has some information on the case."

My heart skips a beat. I follow Trisha into the living room.

Stephen is at the kitchen island, making himself tacos with

the leftovers. He raises his eyebrows at me and then goes back to scooping toppings.

"Well?" I ask.

"I was able to use your justification about the lack of knuckle tattoos to get another search warrant on Bart and Ace's apartment. And like you said, there was a softball bat there." Stephen takes a bite of his taco.

"And?" My heart is racing.

"The bat had blood on it. Bart had cleaned it, but there was still blood in the brushing of the aluminum. That is not the craziest part of this whole thing. In some twisted fashion, you could even say Bart is a victim in this."

Now I am confused. "Somebody used his bat?"

Stephen's face twists. "No. He killed Champ. He told us he crushed his head in with the bat, and for good measure, put two rounds in him with your pistol."

"He admitted that?"

"He laid out everything for us."

"Why was he so cooperative?" I ask.

Stephen looks at his taco longingly. "Easy. He got some unwelcome news today. His girlfriend, Champ's widow, let him know she miscarried his baby today. Bart killed Champ to marry Audrey and start a family. Now he is suspicious he was duped. A tough time to finally get smart, I would say."

"And Ace?"

"Bart did not like him. He figured he would be an easy mark. It was an airtight frame job. Audrey told Champ that Ace hit on her. She claimed he said lewd things about her girl parts and what he wanted to do to her." Stephen gestures with his finger. "That was the fight you broke up with your pistol.

"Then, when Ace got home. Bart lifted his hat, sunglasses, and Blue Angels flight jacket. Guess what Bart found in the coat pocket."

"My forty-five."

"Bingo, your forty-five. So, rather than use the gun he bought for the coup de grâce—remember he invited Ace to the shooting range last weekend—Bart used your forty-five. It was too perfect to pass up."

"Is Ace free?" I ask.

"Not exactly. Ace still must appear in court for the resisting arrest and striking an officer charges."

I had forgotten about those. The police should let it go since Ace was arrested for something he did not do, but the system doesn't work like that.

Stephen waves his hand through the air. "But that is not the bizarre part of this whole story. Are you ready for this?"

I must be grinning like the Cheshire cat. Stephen seems to be eating it up.

"Audrey denies every bit of this."

"After lying to Bart about being pregnant and having a miscarriage, what made you think she would own up to it?" I ask.

"Is she going to get away with it?" Trisha asks.

"We don't have any film footage of her or a weapon tying her into the murder. As far as any jury is concerned, it is her word against Bart's. Unlike Bart, there is no evidence putting her at the murder scene. She has an airtight alibi.

"She was so angry Champ got into the fight she went and spent that night at her girlfriend's. The girlfriend and her mom confirm it."

"Wow, she really did set him up," I say.

"She has probably had practice. She was pregnant when she was sixteen, and her seventeen-year-old lover set her house on fire. It killed her parents, who were asleep inside at the time. She was at a friend's house that night and didn't know anything even though the seventeen-year-old lover swore up and down they agreed on killing her parents so she could marry him." Stephen shakes his head. "She miscarried that baby, too."

I feel dizzy. This explains the complete evil I felt when Audrey entered the bar and why I instantly disliked her. Apparently, I had a psychic event and did not realize it at the time.

"I came by to thank you girls personally. I know I was a little hardheaded this afternoon."

"You were a jerk," I say.

Stephen's eyes open wider as if he is offended. He chuckles. "Yes. I suppose I was a bit difficult. But I would prefer to be skeptical than accidentally put the wrong man in jail."

I let it slide that he had literally done that very thing by incarcerating Ace. The mood is appropriately jovial, and I don't want to rain on the parade.

Chapter 22

The vision only played in my head the one time. It was less than a ten-second event. It was like a bad copy of an old war movie playing briefly before it turned into flames and blurred beyond recognition.

But it has played repeatedly in my head ever since Stephen left.

Norman and Trisha went to bed two hours ago. I'm sitting cross-legged on the sofa, staring at the TV screen—which is off.

Should I have done more? Should I have explained to Wesley my vision of him slumped over the controls of a helicopter in a tailspin?

If I had told him more, I would have been forced to explain my psychic abilities. He would think me crazy—and because he thought I was crazy—he would ignore my warning anyway.

The most aggravating thing of all is I don't even know if it is a warning. The way visions work, it could just be some random scenario that *might* play out. Nothing is necessarily definite. For example, suppose I convinced him to come to Atlanta. He might still fly a traffic helicopter, have a heart attack, and crash the news helicopter. That might be what the vision was revealing.

That is stupid, April. Traffic helicopter pilots do not wear giant helmets and Navy flight suits.

What good are psychic abilities if you can't trust them? That is not fair. My psychic abilities, when dealing with the past, are spot on. It is the visions about the future that are less than reliable.

Why shouldn't they be? Aren't there twenty-five thousand contingency plans playing out in a single day of our life? All of them are based on the smallest of decisions.

I am exhausted, and I don't want to think about it anymore. Unfortunately, my overactive imagination has a hold of it like a junkyard dog with a ham hock.

"You thought you would ignore me."

Even with my legs crossed, somehow I pop six inches into the air. My head jerks toward the voice as a fuzzy, translucent, gray-tone version of Champ appears in the far corner. He walks toward me as I continue to struggle with my new reality.

"I knew you would renege on our deal."

It is incredible how he has almost mastered how to pull together his energy force into a semblance of his old appearance in just a few days. "I've done no such thing, Champ."

He stops at the edge of the sofa. "Give me one good reason I should not strangle you right now."

"I kept my word and solved your murder. That is what you wanted, isn't it? You don't want to walk this earth for all eternity and not know who killed you, do you?"

"Tell me who the coward is."

His anger forces him to lose control, and his appendages turn to smoke again.

"First things first. You must promise never to hurt, check that, never visit Ace or me or anyone in our families again."

"I don't know who all is in your family."

I raise my eyebrows. "Really? I thought you would want to know who killed you."

From his reaction, I would say he does not like how I am talking to him. All but his face has now devolved into swirling black smoke. "You have my word."

"Good." My hands are shaking. I lace them together in front of me. "Bart Neil killed you."

"Who is Bart Neil?"

This is going to hurt. Here we go with the Band-Aid method. "Bart Neil is who Audrey is having an affair with."

The rest of Champ devolves into an undulating black mist except for his eyes. His eyes are a testament to the hatred stoking in his corrupt soul. "I am going to tear his intestines out through his mouth."

I'm not saying I am fond of Bart, and I'm also not sure Champ can make good on his threat. Still, I don't think anybody should die in such a manner. "You should know Bart did the right thing and admitted to your murder. I'm sure he will be put away for an awfully long time. If not the rest of his life. In some ways, he is a victim, too."

"I thought you said he killed me."

"He did. Still, the whole plan was Audrey's idea. She wants your lifestyle, sans you. And honestly, given her checkered past, I'm not sure Bart was going to be around for long, either. I'm not here to tell you what to do, Champ. But I do know if I were in your position, Audrey's who I would hold responsible for your death."

The smoke that is Champ begins to separate and stretch toward the ceiling. As he does, I realize I have signed Audrey's death warrant. As much as she may deserve it, I start to wonder if it makes me an evil person since I turned an angry ghost on an unsuspecting woman.

I will have to live with it. Champ is focused on exacting some sort of revenge for his death. I want to make sure his focus is not on my family or Ace. Some decisions make you feel dirty even when you know they are right.

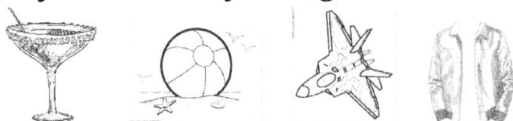

Chapter 23

Trisha and I made rum runners for the beach today. Let me tell you, rum runners on a pristine white beach with my best friend is as close as I can get to heaven this side of the veil.

I feel okay today. Just a notch below fine. I have come to grips with the end of the Lieutenant JG Wesley Greenwood episode of my life.

The rum runners are helping ease the pain. The cut on my heart is still tender, and I expect it will be for a while. Still, I am grateful for the experience. I think it may have awoken a desire inside me that has been dormant while I pushed through my education.

If I don't end up a sixty-year-old career woman who never has a meaningful relationship, I will owe Wesley a debt of gratitude.

Wesley will always hold a unique spot in my heart. I already know that and accept it willingly.

I lean back further in my beach chair and readjust my hat. "What a perfect day."

"Yes, it is," Trisha drawls.

A low rumble rolls across the sand. I squint my eyes looking for the thunderclouds that often pop up in a matter of moments on the Florida Panhandle. Instead, I spy six tiny blue specks on the horizon. Seconds later, the electro-blue F-18 fighter jets scream overhead just a few hundred yards off the coast. My body is electrified with excitement.

Now it is a perfect day.

As I watch the single-engine tails grow smaller, I smile, thinking about my flyboy. The man who, like me, has a goal big enough not to compromise.

You earn your wings and make us proud, Lieutenant JG Greenwood. Then you fly back to me if you have a mind to.

Who knows? Maybe once we have accomplished our goals, you can convince me we can make it work. Stranger things have happened in my life.

The End

Never miss an April May Snow release.

Join the reader's club!

www.mscottswanson.com

Click her to continue Aprils story with,

Throw the Fastball

M. Scott lives outside of Nashville, Tennessee, with his wife and two guard chihuahuas. When he's not writing, he's cooking or taking long walks to smooth out plotlines for the next April May Snow adventure.

Dear Reader,

Thank you for reading April's story. You make her adventures possible. Without you, there would be no point in creating her story.

I'd like to encourage you to post a review on Amazon. A favorable critique from you is a powerful way to support authors you enjoy. It allows our books to be found by additional readers, and frankly, motivates us to continue to produce books. This is especially true for your independents.

Once again, thank you for the support. You are the magic that breathes life into these characters.

M. Scott Swanson

The best way to stay in touch is to join the reader's club!

www.mscottswanson.com

Other ways to stay in touch are:

Like on Amazon

Like on Facebook

Like on Goodreads

You can also reach me at mscottswanson@gmail.com.

I hope your life is filled with

magic and LOVE!

Printed in Great Britain
by Amazon